ALCY LEYVA

AND THEN THERE WERE DRAGONS

ISBN print 978-1-7329357-8-5

epub – 978-1-7335994-0-5

mobi – 978-1-7329357-9-2

Cover design by Najla Qamber

Edited by Squid & Ink

Interior design layout by Rebecca Poole

Map Illustrated by R.H. Stewart

Publication date July 30, 2019

Black Spot Books

First Circle
Second Circle
Third Circle
Fourth Circle
Fifth Circle
Sixth Circle
Seventh Circle
Eighth Circle
Ninth Circle

EPISODE FOUR:

EVERY HELL NEEDS AN OLIVE GARDEN

Back when we were kids, when I was twelve and Petty was eight or nine, we would play this game. We'd steal an old, empty box from the corner bodega—one that smelled like overripe bananas and sported brown stains on the sides from whatever had leaked (or died) in there—and we'd go sledding down the stairs in our building.

I know. Sit in awe of our genius.

On one specific attempt in our makeshift box-sled—one in which I guess I should have zigged rather than zagged—I ended up flying right out of the damn thing and down an entire flight of stairs. After sticking the landing (with my face), I sat up to find that out of five of the fingers on my right hand, one was pointing directly back at my face.

Petty instantly lost her shit. She threw both of her little hands in the air and, with her mouth wailing like a fire truck, started running around in circles like the world was on fire. I opted instead to merely snap the sucker back into place and wrap it in duct tape until my mom got home.

This is all to say I've never been the "get-the-shit-scared-out-of-you-so-bad-you-scream-your-head off" type. I've also never been the dead type, so you can imagine all of this was uncharted territory for me.

You can't blame me for screaming. One second, I'm bleeding out on the steps of Saint Patrick's Cathedral on Fifth Avenue in Manhattan. The next, I'm waking up in a bed that isn't mine, in a strange room I've never seen before. Oh, and the cherry on top of this perfectly-served dung sundae? I've found myself laying a few feet from none other than

Gaffrey-fucking-Palls, the man solely responsible for uprooting my sad little existence and dumping it into a gutter.

So, yeah, the situation begged for a hefty dose of delirious panic. And boy, did I deliver.

I screamed my fucking head off.

When I was through, Palls grimaced and smacked his lips. "Nice to see you, too, Grey."

Wasting no time, I pushed the covers aside and swung my feet over just enough to make sure I didn't touch that scum-sucker in the slightest. It quickly dawned on me that my surroundings were not the only things out of the ordinary.

I was wearing a dress.

I know—a *dress*!

It wasn't just any dress, either. It was a black dress with lace netting around the neck and arms. The bottom was layered with grey and black material, which billowed outward like smoke around my bare feet. I looked like I had been invited to a prom for the recently deceased—or at least the Halloween costume version of said event.

Pushing through my current coma-induced fashion sense, I spotted a chair on the other side of the room, parked by what appeared to be a writing desk topped with a green ornate lamp. I marked this as my target and pushed away from the bed, but the moment my feet hit the carpet, my world toppled over. I saw the ceiling, the velvet-like wallpaper and empty picture frames hanging on the wall, and then nothing but plush carpet as I flopped right over onto the floor like a fat, waterlogged sponge.

Palls sighed as he watched me slump onto the ground. "Yeah. Might need to take it easy for a bit there, Grey. You still don't have your—"

I slung him a tight *shhh* to cease and desist his bullshit. My arms and legs felt like wet noodles, but giving up was not an option and so I began inching myself across the ground, all chin and stomach and shoulders, like a grub.

Watching me struggle, Palls decided to start talking.

"I realize this is probably a 'crap the bed' moment for you." He rubbed his forehead with the back of his hand like he was trying to wipe away that particularly bothersome mental image and continued. "I'm going to try to make this all clear and simple, so let's start from the obvious and make our way down. By now, you've probably figured out where we are. This is Hell and you're stuck down here for all of the crazy stunts you pulled back in your life—the Shades, the quasi-end of the world, etcetera. That's the bad news."

Palls paused. My time as a worm had come to an end. There was energy bubbling up; my limbs were waking, coming to life. Palls watched as I propped myself on my elbows and twerked my ass forward until the momentum forced me up and into the chair. I was out of breath and sweat was running in streams down my back. When I was done wriggling to a more or less upright position, he continued.

"Now for the *really* bad news. Your soul, like mine, is bound to this place. That's why you're feeling sluggish right now. Heard them call it 'soul entropy' and it's pretty common for folks who end up here. See, you don't have a body, per se. It's more like your soul's been hotwired to feel extreme emotions, pain and fear especially. You'll learn to get used to it, but that's why you're having such a hard time using your legs. You probably can't move your mouth just yet either, which is good for me because I heard you typically have a problem keeping it shut. You're used to using your muscles to feel and get around, but that's mortality for you—that's *real* life. Nothing's 'real' down here. Well, other than the endless suffering. Oh, and the awful sulfur smell, but that's either the lake of fire or the Olive Garden they opened one floor up. Can't really be sure one way or the next. I guess making our souls run on pain makes it easier for everlasting torture and whatnot. Gives them something to screw around with."

Palls stopped again as I finally managed to work my way onto my feet. Each of my knees took turns wobbling as I forced myself into a standing position using the backrest of the desk chair. It felt like life was welling up inside of me again, though I was pretty sure my surroundings would beg to differ. Slowly, and with every ounce of strength I had, I started pushing the chair toward Palls.

When I was close enough to be satisfied, I plopped myself right down onto the chair's cushion and stared at him for a long minute. Gaffrey

Palls: the man who had tried to murder me. The man who had walked into my apartment full of demonic crows I would unknowingly release out into the world.

The man who had started this whole shit show.

My "body" (or whatever version of it this was) seemed to be waking up slowly, but there was a dull hollowness to it all. I could grab the round of my knee and lick my lips, but it felt like senses running on a separate track from my skin—like I was divorced from everything my body was trying to tell me and experiencing it all from memory. Somehow, sitting there, I felt as if I were planted in that chair and completely outside of my body at exactly the same time.

I lifted my right hand. The last time I remember using it was right before the sword of the psychotic Seraphim, Barnem, severed it. He had been using me, manipulating all my family and friends, just so he could move the expiration date of mankind forward a few centuries—just so he could do his fucking job. That's right. My life—and everyone's around me—went to shit because of one guy feeling "less-than" in the job security department. Sure, I managed to stop him, but it had come with a price: not only did I lose my arm but I had also lost my younger sister, Petty—lost her twice, as a matter of fact. I had also lost the only guy who had ever been nice to me, though Donaldson was a complete dork most of the time. And, I had lost my soul, too. I had a Shade inside of me—a demon, a ticking time bomb. Maybe it had been there my entire life? I don't know. I never got any good answers.

Palls sighed again. "Alright, Grey. What do you have to say? Out with it."

I held up the hand I thought I had lost. I curled each finger, flexed each digit.

Then I formed one mighty fist and parked that son of a bitch right on the side of Gaffrey Palls' face, squarely between his jaw and cheekbone. I put all of my weight behind it—every bit of rage, all my hatred and fury was wrapped around my fist like barbed wire.

For being such a big guy, the blow was surprisingly strong enough to send Palls tumbling from the bed, ass over hat, like an old sack of laundry.

He landed behind the bed and slouched against the wall, his black hair flopping into the impact mark of my knuckles.

The sensation of the punch—the feeling of flesh meeting skull—surged up from my fist and manifested itself, blowing out into every corner of the room like wildfire. The air around us shook like someone had struck a twenty-foot bell with a baseball bat. The resulting pain in my own "body" felt amplified by several degrees and spliced by at least three commas as it tore through my arm like an explosion of thorns and nearly threatened to split me apart in the process. But, even through the tears in my eyes, I breathed through it, reveled in the splash of violence. I stood there, panting, *praying* his face felt a hundred times worse than what was vibrating in my arm and shoulder.

"Okay, Palls," I said with a smile, returning to a comfy seated position. "Run all of that by me again. I wasn't paying attention."

Palls blinked. "Alright, Grey. I told you everything … again. You still think this is necessary?"

I thought about it for a second. "Yup."

While he had been lying on the floor, dazed by my haymaker, I had looked for things to restrain him. Unfortunately, Gaffrey Palls was built like an ice cream truck and nothing in the room looked useful. Making do with what I had, I had dragged the bed over his body and slammed the frame over his torso. I also dumped whatever furniture I could manage on top of that—the desk, the chair, the dresser—to effectively pin the bastard to the ground. I even sat on the edge of the mattress and dangled my legs menacingly where his face stared up at the bottoms of my feet.

"I feel like we need to establish a few guidelines," I informed my ensnared victim.

In my head, I knew this was not a good look for me. I could completely understand how someone walking into that room and spotting me sitting atop a mountain of furniture, which was, at that very moment, pinning down another human being might totally get people to thinking I was overreacting. Just a bit. Just a *tad*.

Then again, this was Gaffrey Palls we are talking about. I was not taking any chances.

Also, history proves most people don't know shit.

"I told you everything, Grey." Pall's voice sounded squeezed beneath all the furniture.

Crossing my legs, I propped an elbow on my knee and settled my chin on my fist. "Right. But, I don't believe anything you have to say so..."

Even with all of the weight crushing down on his chest, Palls managed to look bored. "So, you don't believe me when I say what this place is?"

"Oh, no. I believe this is Hell. I mean, you're here," I said flexing the arm I shouldn't have had. "And trust me. I've lived my life these past few months hearing what my final destination was. Plus, I think I've seen weirder shit than a dingy hotel room."

Palls rolled his eyes. "I figured you might be hardheaded, but this really takes the cake. Why would I lie to you?"

Seething, I leaned over to look him right in the face and spit my reply. "Oh, I don't know. How about that time you tried to kill me in my own apartment? Pretty sure attempted murder is the kind of thing that would put a strain on our relationship."

"But you killed *me*," Palls shot back.

"When in Rome."

I knew the retort didn't make sense in context, but I was flustered and wanted the last word. Luckily, Palls let me have it.

"I got something else to tell you," Palls said. "Something that might help our trust issues."

"Wait." I leapt down from the wreckage, grabbed another chair, tossed it on top of the rest, and re-perched myself. "Continue."

"Your sister is here."

Those four words landed like four point-blank cannon blasts to my chest. My shoulders slumped; my spine bent in on itself and forced me to slouch over. I felt like someone had filled my guts with hot mud. Then I remembered Palls had mentioned something about our bodies being in tune with pain and misery, and it all came to me. It was your typical hurt-resentment-fear-shame cocktail, only amped up so high it felt like I was the one pinned under two tons of crappy hotel furniture. The weight seemed to come at me from all directions—from every cell and bone and hair follicle.

After calming myself, I took a breath. "You're lying."

"I'm not," Palls retorted. "She's here. In the hotel."

"Shut up."

"I've been keeping her safe."

"Shut—"

"Grey, I can take you to Petunia."

"Don't you fucking say her name!" I shouted and Palls froze. Feeling as if I had to stay in control, I gave myself a few light slaps—the kind meant to wake yourself up instead of inflicting any real pain. The sting of it helped me focus enough to sit up and center myself. "I don't know what your game is, Palls, but you almost had me there. You almost made me slip. There's no way Petty's here. The agreement I made with those freakish angels was supposed to take care of her."

Palls tossed me a look like I had tried to lecture him about the existence of the Tooth Fairy. "Not sure if you've been paying attention at all, Grey, but angels aren't exactly folks you should keep on the honor system."

He had a point and—I had to admit—I hated him even more for it. I looked up at the door and chose my next words *very* carefully. "So you're saying I'm in Hell?"

"That's what I'm saying."

"And Petty's here?"

Palls rolled his eyes. "Yes."

"And your advice is that I, under no circumstances, leave this room?"

"I wouldn't advise you to, no." There was a long pause and Palls sighed. "You're going to do it anyway, aren't you? Even though I told you not to?"

"No, Palls," I laughed as I hopped off the bed and walked toward the doorknob. "I'm going to do it *because* you told me not to. Major difference."

Palls immediately started trying to struggle his way out from beneath all the junk I'd piled on him, but before he could wrestle himself free, I flung open the door and stepped through.

At first, the hallway looked more or less like a typical hotel hallway. The ceilings were lined with mirrors punctuated by full-bodied

chandeliers that cast a reddish tint on everything. Like in the room, the walls were fashioned with empty pictures frames, some larger than my body. That's where it started to get…strange. Also scattered in tiny nooks, outcrops, and shelves where cats, hundreds of them, quietly snoozing as if they owned the place. There were so many prowling the hallway I had to step over a few to avoid tripping. Not one of the lazy fur balls paid me any mind as I made my way past.

Every few feet the hallway was interrupted by identical wooden doors positioned directly across from each other like mirror reflections. Each one was fastened shut but I could hear, very faintly, murmuring behind each of the wooden panels. Sometimes I heard a gurgle of music, sometimes splatters of laughter wafting around the open hallways, but never once did I see another soul—besides the cats. The entire hotel seemed completely abandoned, but only in the same sense that a haunted house advertised its vacancy.

A few steps in and I already felt like I had been walking this hallway for hours without an end in sight. What's more is there was a sense of dread rising in my chest. The lighting in the hallway was off somehow, casting shadows where there shouldn't be any. Listening to the murmurs around me and with no exit in sight, I suddenly grew afraid of the doors and their stillness, of the mouths and hands and bodies creating the sounds on the other side of their closed panels. More than anything, it felt like my nerves were screaming through a bullhorn that danger was approaching. I imagined Palls would come bursting out of one of the rooms and try to strangle me—again—and this time, he wouldn't stop. My tongue would sag out of my mouth. My eyes would burst out of my head. He'd kill me like I had killed him.

The panic became so real I started to run. The ominous voices circling in my head were quickly swallowed up by the sounds of my breath leaving my lips, my black dress swishing around my knees, and my footsteps thudding against the gaudy carpet. I went from a run to a sprint, and then a sprint to an all out "fuck-all-this" scramble.

I passed door after door, leapt over one feline after another, but the hallway wouldn't end. It *couldn't* end. It just kept going and going. I was

trapped in the impossible. There were no windows, no explanation of the outside world. Just an endless corridor of disembodied voices.

Then came a sound.

One above the rest.

Heavy footsteps.

Palls was in pursuit.

One moment I was walking down some freaky hallway, the next I found myself in the worst sort of waking nightmare imaginable. There was no other way to describe it. I was trapped in a slasher movie where no matter how fast the victim ran, the maniac *always* caught up. *Always* with little effort. For a second, I considered stopping, standing my ground, and giving Palls another taste of a Queens-bred sucker punch.

But then, out of nowhere, a bell sounded.

It was a chime of the small, annoying, tinkling variety—the kind overweight kings used to summon their fools when they needed another piece of food or some entertainment. Or the kind obnoxious posh people used to call for their Botox refills. A bell no bigger than my hand. But, regardless of how teeny the tinkling sounded, it managed to sweep through the hallway like a dark pulse of energy. The floorboards started creaking, the chandeliers flickered. I couldn't shake the feeling the hotel itself had only been sleeping before and this chime was its wake-up call. I felt dark eyes crawling all over me, hands moving through the shadows. Now this place was ready to bare its teeth.

Looking behind me, I saw the bell had stopped Palls cold, too. He was dressed differently. On top of his black suit, he now wore a dirty trench coat and matching fedora. He also wore the face of someone scared out of his wits. Terror had crept into his eyes—absolute terror—as Gaffrey Palls stared down the hallway toward the source of the light jingle.

"We need to go. *Now*!" he yelled and reached out to grab me, but as he did all the doors in the hallway spontaneously burst open. The entire hallway was flooded with hundreds of people, like a dam of humanity had broken. Twenty people poured out of the room closest to me alone. There was such a large mass of bodies that I quickly found myself overwhelmed and caught in their herded footsteps. Palls reached out to grab me again,

but I ducked away from his fingers and went with the flow. While I didn't like the thought of getting swallowed up by this congregation, I knew I could use it to get some distance between that nut-job and me.

The army of hotel patrons wore suits and dresses of every shade of red. The men boasted crimson tuxedos, wine-colored three-piece suits with dangling watchstraps and fedoras, and loud candy apple zoot suits. The women sported cocktail dresses with plumes arching off of them like scarlet ostriches, dazzling 20's era dresses with ruby colored tassels, and dresses with material overlapping even more material until it all exploded outward through the neckline as if attempting the fashion equivalent of an erupting volcano.

The mass seemed completely unaware that Palls and I were standing there as they pushed into us on their way down the hall. He and I instantly lost sight of each other as they bumped, shoved, and pushed through us. I thought I heard Palls call out to me, but a tall, svelte woman wearing red netting around her face and a raspberry lampshade dress collided with me. I tried shoving her back, but I might as well have tried to push over a parked car. She just gripped a half-lit cig in her ruby lips as she knocked me backward with each forward step.

The well-dressed horde marched down the hallway, swerving into a large hall with a wooden table that was long enough to seat the hundreds of murmuring souls as its centerpiece. Four massive fireplaces stood on each side of the room, each one sculpted into a howling demon's face. Between them, and taking up almost every inch of wall space, was a litany of animal heads: bucks, moose, lions, sharks, bulls. It was like someone had gunned down, skinned, and mounted every animal Noah had managed to bum a ride to.

The hotel patrons stopped pushing and took their seats. From where I was standing, I couldn't see either end of the table and there was absolutely no sign of Palls. Not knowing what else to do, I took a seat to blend in and buy myself some time.

Suddenly, and with great zeal, out came a small battalion of marionette waiters— wooden servants without strings. Red and white uniforms were painted directly on their carved skins. They held silver trays raised

above their heads on flat hands. Upon reaching the tables, the waiters swooped their platters down in front of the diners, removing the serving domes with ridiculous bravado.

All manner of food came spilling out: baked turkeys with vegetables, diced lamb chunks, succulent steaks over diced potatoes. There was more food than the trays themselves could fit, and most of the dishes rolled out onto the gold tablecloth with very little disregard for presentation.

The people immediately stopped talking and started eating. They stabbed at the meats with forks and piled slabs of meat onto their dinner plates. Still unsatisfied, they grabbed at fruits and vegetables and donuts and diced ham chunks with their bare hands.

With everyone focused entirely on their meals, I pushed back in my chair and looked both ways, like a hesitant pedestrian about to cross a raging highway. With Palls a no-show, I slipped out of my chair and started looking for an exit, pushing my way deeper into the room and hoping to find another door. No one tried to stop me. No one even seemed to notice me.

Creeping further and further backward, I began to notice the sound of people eating— lips smacking, full guttural swallows—was extremely loud and growing louder. What had started as a buzz was swelling into a panic. I wasn't sure if it was a trick of the light, but as I stared at the feasting souls I got the impression their hands and mouths had begun to move faster, to blur and smear across their faces so that their moving mouths looked less like mouths and more like angry red blurs. The sounds of their hunger echoed throughout the room as they stuffed more and more food into their face-holes.

Within minutes it was a full-on frenzy. Patrons kicked over chairs. Some climbed onto the table and began grabbing lobsters and cakes and omelets with their hands and biting into them, sending shells and crumbs and bits—and possibly teeth—sprinkling everywhere.

What had started off as a dinner had evolved into a full-blown riot and I sure as hell didn't feel like sticking around. Breaking into a run, I vaulted over two men fighting over steamed sea bass and hockey-checked an older woman salting a turkey leg (not because she was in my way, but because I was in the mood).

As I fought my way through the crowd, something came over me. A sensation. A warmth. I wanted to stop. I wanted to sit and eat. I was hungry—starving, as a matter of fact.

I wanted to have a meal.

I *needed* to.

My sprint turned into a trot—and then without deciding to, I came up short.

Just one bite of savory turkey leg, I thought to myself, and my hand reached out at the last one on a serving tray. Luckily, I was moving sluggishly enough to see the fork aimed at my hand and avoid it. A man in a ruby tuxedo and a red horned half-mask swiveled to face me. His mouth opened and spittle flew from his lips as he hissed like a rabid animal. In one hand, he held a silver serving tray, in the other, a bent fork. Just before he lunged at me, his neighbor—a woman in a fitted skirt that looked as if it was made from the husk of a grapefruit—stabbed him in the side of the head with her carving knife. The force sent his lifeless body sprawling into the center of the table, the pointy end of the knife pinning his corpse directly to the wood.

That's when the real madness of the dinner party spread. No longer content with the bounty in front of them, the hotel guests turned on each other. With knives and teeth and nails, the meal turned into a slaughter. They started *eating* each other.

One woman, steak knives in hand, stood on her seat and leapt at me. Her eyes were crazed, her mouth drooling in buckets.

I picked up the silver serving tray the dead guy had dropped and swung it upward at her head. With the loud sound of a gong, the blow shattered her mask and sent her body spiraling into a small group of people huddled over the bloody remains of what used to be a man who was himself too into his potpie to realize he was being eaten.

Without a second to breathe, a second man leapt onto my back. Before I could toss him off, Palls' fist came out of nowhere and plowed into the man's body with a sick crunch that sent him flying into the starving masses. Palls grabbed me by the wrist and—because there was nothing more important than getting the hell out of there at the moment—I let him and we ran.

I'm not sure how we managed to get out of that horror, but when we finally jumped through the door, we stumbled into the thin hallway and collapsed onto the floor.

Shaking and emotionally exhausted, I felt like my body wouldn't let me move an inch. We were back out onto the infinite hallway, but everything was different. The lights on the chandeliers were red, tinging everything in the dark stain of blood red. The walls of the hallway even looked tighter, more cramped. It didn't help that the army of cats that had previously been running around the place now seemed scared shitless too, mewing pitifully as they scattered in all directions.

Palls was staring at something coming at us from down the hallway. He staggered to his feet and quickly pulled me to mine.

"Well, we're screwed," he groaned. "The Warden's here."

"Who?"

A round ball of rippling black shadow too big for the tight space rolled toward us like a dark marble down a hungry throat. Unable to fit properly, it scraped against the walls, crushing doors and frames and trampling a few cats as its mass heaved in our direction. The darkness of its shadow swallowed everything up as it drew near.

Palls didn't move. Neither did I. We stood our ground

From out of the darkness, a thin tear formed at the center of the shadow. Greasy black blood splashed onto the carpeting like an invisible claw had ruptured some sort of dank, rotten artery. In its wake, a figure spilled into the hallway. It was a tall creature with a long black beak, swathed in dark robes. With one gloved hand on a cane sporting a crow's head and the other tucked behind its back, the figure stood with what could only be described as an absolute dick-ish posture. Pulling on the black beak, the figure moved his mask away to expose a man's smirking mouth.

"Now-now, Grey," Mason Scarborough called in his usual snobbish drawl, "one mustn't leave before dessert. That would be *rude*."

I DIDN'T NEED to think too hard to recall the shitload of grief Mason Scarborough (aka Captain Cross) had given me back when the two of us were still alive.

He was much taller than the last time I had seen him, longer and lankier-looking, too. Mason's robe swelled and settled into a slim, European-cut suit as he took a step toward us: black blazer, purple shirt, black tie—dude looked like a bruised eggplant. His white hair was tied back into a tight man-bun, which only worked to promote his overwhelming douchery.

Palls attempted to grab my wrist again but I backhanded him squarely in his throat and stepped forward. Smoothing down my dress, I turned to our newest arrival and feigned a hearty, "Masonnnnn! I almost didn't recognize you. Oh, right. Maybe it's because the last time we saw each other you were being impaled by a giant demon parrot. Ah, the good 'ol days!"

He scowled so hard I thought his face had turned to stone. Mason always looked like it was personally draining to have to deal with other human beings, a habit he hadn't lost being dead. In many ways, I could relate.

"I see you still have that mouth of yours, Grey. It means so much to me that, even in Hell, you still seem to serve as the epicenter to my waking misery."

"Compliment," I said, batting my eyelashes.

Mason turned his attention to Palls. "Never took you as one for charity, Gaffrey."

Rising to his full height, Palls loomed over both of us, and yet didn't seem to have a violent bone in his corporeal body. "We're leaving, Mason," he said, flexing his neck around the painful lump where my hand had landed.

"Leaving?" Mason stamped his cane on the ground for emphasis. "Don't act as if you have any jurisdiction down here, Gaffrey. And besides, we're just catching up. Birds of a feather and at all that. I hope you don't forget who has the true authority in this hotel." Turning to me, Mason continued, "You know, when I first saw the name 'Grey' written in for a reservation, I will admit I became quite giddy. Just the thought of having you here to dismember, decapitate, and disembowel, night after night until the end of time, well, I saw it as a valuable 'pick-me-up' during my dark days." Mason laughed and it was just as horrible as you would think—it sounded like someone had lashed three cats together by their tails using barbed wire and launched them down a flight of stairs.

After the bizarre screeching, his face grew serious. "Imagine my disappointment when it was *Petunia* Grey standing before me and not her dear older sister."

Hearing Petty's name was a trigger, but the fear overtaking me at that moment was unlike anything I had ever felt before. Honestly, I couldn't get a handle on anything I was feeling. It was as if I was being bombarded by every color and sound in the spectrum, each of them fighting for screen time in my mind until they blended together in a chaotic swirl of noise and static. There were all there, but nothing made sense.

Mason brandished his crow-headed cane and a black ball of sludge shot from its tip, slamming into Palls and me and pinning us against the wall. The goo was as strong as cement, but it felt like something alive as it undulated and churned like a thousand hands pressing against my body.

"It feels like centuries since I've seen your face, Grey," Mason growled, drawing so close I could taste his hatred where his breath hit my skin. "And all of this time, I've fantasized about the moment you would be in front of me again. Seeing your sister show up instead was more than just

a buzz kill—but I do remember her. Oh, I do. And torturing her, teaching her some respect, was something I was anticipating."

Struggling against the goo holding me captive, I shouted, "Leave her alone, Mason. She doesn't belong here. She didn't do anything to you. She's innocent!"

Mason Scarborough's eyes drained of anything that resembled life and when he spoke again his voice was flat, each word sparking as it lit from his tongue.

"She shot me in the head."

I stopped struggling as the memory came to back to me.

"Oh, right...well, I think we can all agree two out of three isn't bad. I think that's fair."

"Your mouth won't get you out of this, Grey."

"No, but this will," Palls shouted as one of his fists burst out of the black shadow and decked Mason in the chest. The fist itself was bound in a shadowy bonfire of black fire. The force from the blow blasted Mason down the hallway, where he vanished into thin air.

I didn't have time to dwell on the freakish nature of what I had just seen as Palls tore my restraints away. The remaining goo wriggled like a black tongue when it hit the floor, sliding down the hall after the mouth it belonged to.

Gross.

"We need to go. That won't keep him down for long." Palls had barely gotten the sentence out when Mason reappeared, stepping out of a black tear and this time accompanied by four masked figures in red tuxedos.

"I was going to ask you to stay for dinner," he said, now speaking as if all the fun had gone out of the whole situation. "*That* was me being considerate. But now, I'm just going to lop off your limbs and use your skin as drapes in my private study. For this task, I have chosen my most trusted and vicious concierge—a being whose thirst for blood and carnage has even given *me* pause from time to time. It will not stop pursuing you until you have been mashed into paste—until you are crushed and maimed beyond comprehension. Until your warm guts fill up into your mouth like..."

As Mason monologued the more gruesome details of our certain dismemberment, one of the masked men—one who looked like a fiery red parrot—leaned over and whispered something into his ear.

"What do you mean Steve has the day off?" Mason snapped.

The masked man leaned back into his ear and whispered again.

The Warden gnashed his teeth. "I know what it *means* to have a day off, you idiot." Mason ran a gloved hand over his face. "Fine, fine. Who's left?"

Another masked man produced a clipboard and presented it to his boss. Mason turned to page two, and then page three. Four. "Okay, next manager's meeting, we'll be discussing this coverage issue. Everyone wants to take off before a long weekend. And I don't care if he has a century of personal days saved up. Now I have to send the new girl from the temp agency. It's downright unprofessional."

A ball of fire blossomed between us as a being emerged from the flames. It wore a black hooded robe with small skulls lining its belt, which managed to look unimpressively goth around here. The black mask covering its face sported a long, sharp snout, resembling some sort of canine. Its slender fingers outstretched and an enormous silver hammer appeared in its hand. Most of the metal was painted in sporadic blood splatter. Not a great welcome sight, but decidedly effective.

Palls grabbed my wrist again. "We need to get out of here, Grey. We can't win this fight."

I flicked his grasp away. "First of all, you need to stop grabbing me. Second…" I stepped up to the being with the gruesome hammer and cracked my neck. This figure stood over six feet tall, but I made sure not to back down. "Look at what I'm wearing, Palls. There's no way I'm dying in a dress."

Two more masked figures joined ranks with the hooded torturer. Behind me, Palls followed suit, standing at my back like we were sorting ourselves into teams for a schoolyard game.

"Don't remember asking for help," I snapped, though I secretly enjoyed the thought of having the psychopath in my corner for once. This was a numbers game.

The two groups stared at each other for a few seconds.

With lightning-fast hands, the cloaked figure reached out and grabbed me by the neck. Before I could break the hold, it shoved me down and swung the massive hammer past my head. Its momentum swung into an upturn, and with a deadly radial spin, crashed against the masked men at its back. Their bodies burst like water balloons on contact, and in one slick movement the hooded figure jackknifed the hammer at Mason's head, hooked both Palls and me by the arms, and dashed down the hall with us in tow like a bolt of lightning carrying a couple of wayward comets.

The hallway was a blur as we moved at such a speed that our legs dangled in the wind like kite tails. Suddenly, we stopped and I heard the ding and rusted metal slide of an elevator door. The figure tossed us inside, and quickly joined us, shutting the gate behind it.

Looking through the gate, I watched as the hallway started to warp and buckle. The lights exploded, the walls crumbled, and screams spilled from every room and corner. With his suit torn, his white man-bun blowing in the wind, and a fancy new pair of black wings sprouting from his back, Mason Scarborough was flying towards us with pure madness in his eyes.

With perfect timing, the elevator cleared the floor before he arrived, ending the sound of my name being screamed from his lips with a nice muting *pop*.

Palls and I, having both managed to scramble to our feet, drew backward to the walls of the elevator as the hooded figure turned and lowered its hood. Blonde hair spilled out and the figure leaned back so that her head thumped against the wall.

"Why is it so hard to keep a job?" she asked, and I assumed it was rhetorical. The woman was out of breath and sweating. Rolling her face to the side so she could see us clearly, she shook her head and winked at me. "Take it easy there, gorgeous. I won't bite."

It took a blink, but then I recognized her. It was a little bit of a delayed reaction, but the low lighting (not to mention the crazed maniac we had just escaped) had rattled my memory loose. The moment her face finally registered on my timeline, I couldn't help but yell at her.

"Cain! What are you doing here?"

"You know each other?" Palls asked.

"Hi, Grey." Cain—the woman I knew as a former angel of death—slid to the ground in a deep, full body exhale. "Small afterlife, eh?"

Suddenly, the consequence of our escape hit me. "Wait! Petty! We left Petty down there." I looked for a switch to stop the doors, but there wasn't one. "We need to go back down." I swiveled to Palls. He bowed his head as if to ward off the shout that was coming next, but I delivered it anyway. It was deafening in the small space. "I am not leaving without my sister! You said she was down there and I am *not* leaving her behind!"

"Your cute sister isn't down there," Cain butted in. She had wrestled her way out of the dark robe and slammed it into the ground with disgust. Without the hooded ensemble, she looked more or less like she had when I last seen her: dressed simply in a black t-shirt and black jeans that were ripped at the knees. "She was, but she's not anymore."

"Where did she go?" Palls stole my line.

"Summoned up to Limbo."

"Who called?"

"Dunno," Cain finished, letting the rest of her hair down and combing it through with her fingers. "Of course, Mason was pisssssssed," she said, turning the last word up several thousand octaves with its own crescendo. She smiled triumphantly, as if this little performance brought her some sliver of joy.

"All right! That's it!" I had had enough. I stood there seething. Gaffrey Palls and Cain the ex-god of death/ex-torturer in hell both seemed shocked I'd bulldozed my way back into the conversation, which had originally been *mine*. "I'm tired of people talking around me. I'm tired of not knowing what the fuck is going on. I'm tired of people making plans about me as if this isn't impacting my life or *after*life or whatever. I want to know what's going on and I want to know *now*!"

All I got back was silence. The elevator was rising slowly, but there was no humming mechanism or dull engine to narrate our movement. We were just quietly skimming upward through a dark shaft blanketed in shadows. It dawned on me that the space between the floors of the hotel seemed ages apart. What elevator takes this long just to go up one level?

"It's not easy to explain," Palls offered, but I quickly shut that shit down.

"Try me."

Cain laughed. "You're still so adorable, Grey. Can't say I approve of the company you're currently keeping, but who am I to judge?" She rolled onto her knees and stood to her feet, but instead of answering me, she looked straight up. "All right. I'm down to talk and tell you everything I know—just not now. We're almost at the Second Circle. I'd think twice about yapping too loud when we get there."

The elevator took a bump and shook. It seemed we were arriving at our destination.

Palls sighed. He crossed his arms over his thick chest and closed his eyes as if in meditation. "Can she borrow that robe?" he asked, referring to Cain's old employee uniform.

Cain shrugged and handed it to me.

I took the garb from her, mouthed a thank you since it was probably the nice thing to do, and promptly threw the thing in Palls' face. "Why do I have to put this on?"

Palls tapped each of his fat fingers on his arm as the robe slipped off his face and returned to its former position on the floor. "You said you want answers, but you also heard your…friend. We need to stay out of people's eyeballs, especially on this next level. Plus, this bit can be a lot to take in when it's your first time."

I clapped my hands together and shouted. "O-kay. Let's get something straight. Before I got down here, I was doing just fine. Sure, things got a little hairy, but I went up against a deranged angel *and* five demons. Five! And, let's not forget, I saved the world."

"Weren't you the reason it was ending in the first place?" Cain interjected.

I nodded slowly. "All right. Okay. If you want to be a Negative Nancy about it, sure. I'm personally more of a 'world half-saved' person, but whatever. Big picture: I went up against the forces of evil and I won."

"You died," Palls chimed in.

"A technicality. Look, my point is: this isn't my first fiery rodeo. I've vanquished evil—several, in fact. I've stared right into the face of adversity and burped into it. You can keep your robes. You can keep your advice and coddling. I'm pretty sure I can handle a crazy hotel full of cannibals. In my sleep. *On laundry day*!"

The elevator stopped suddenly and Cain pulled back the gate without adding anything to my speech. She walked through and Palls gestured I should step out before him. I walked out of the lift, not out into another hallway, but into a street.

A street that ran for miles into a valley of buildings.

Buildings harvested together and dotted by shadowed skyscrapers.

Skyscrapers so high they seemed to rake the very sky itself.

I had walked out onto a city a layman might mistake for the New York I left behind. There were hundreds of people around us: hot dog vendors, knock-off purse dealers, crosswalk cops. They were walking along the sidewalk or waiting to cross at streetlights; they honked their car horns with disgust in what looked like the thick of rush hour traffic. I even spotted some people running for a rattling elevated train that was snaking its way in and out of the city skyline.

But this wasn't New York—this wasn't the city I grew up in and learned to love and to hate. The big freaking red flag for this truth was the people walking by us—these *people* heading to their cubicles and retail spaces and antique umbrella stores—were not people. In fact, they weren't human at all.

They had purple and red skins, and scales. They had spaded tails and large forking horns. Some breathed fire, some were *on* fire. They wore suits and loincloths and held their coffee cups with talons or black lobster claws. There were non-humans the size of trucks that shook the pavement when they walked, and others fluttered about on wings that flapped so quickly they blurred as they hovered in place. The only thing even remotely human about them was their phone use. Most of these creatures were on their phones. Scratch that—*everyone* was on their phones.

Palls walked a few feet ahead, stopped, and silently offered me the robe again.

Without an ounce of protest, I took the garment and pulled my head through the hood.

As I peered out at this vast metropolis filled to the brim with every demon and monster imaginable, I heard Palls say, "Welcome to New Necropolis, Amanda Grey."

"AHHHHH. FEELS FUCKING great to let the girls out after a long day's work!" Cain yelled.

Totally expecting something else, I watched two black-feathered wings shoot out of her shoulder blades and spread out in one glorious arc. She stretched and preened them for a few seconds before folding them neatly behind her back.

Palls and Cain made me walk between them as we made our way through the city of Necropolis. And, keeping to their word, our journey was more or less "weird free." Or, at the very least, it was "weird lite" considering I was trekking through Hell with an angel and a dead murderer. Staying off of the main streets, we moved through the city quickly.

The hood over my face made it hard to see much. Cain told me hiding my face was for my own protection, but something told me there were things they didn't want me to see, too. I'll admit, part of me was grateful for this.

From the bits and pieces I did see on my short jog, New Necropolis was just like my hometown: folks arguing about rent swells, air that sometimes smelled like food and sometimes like bodily fluids, fistfights about parking spaces. Sure, these were demons carrying out these New York staples, but it still managed to remind me of Home Sweet Home.

Not to play into the whole ambience thing, but the devil was truly in the details in New Necro. The little touches—the creepy details that coated everything with a sinister sheen of rotting paint—that were, by far, the toughest to block out. Whether it be the advertisements on certain buildings promoting tools for skin carvings, or the bizarre street names (a notable standout being when we had to wait on the corner of Adolf and Inquisition Boulevard), this city was truly a hellscape. But, while the ads themselves had their own problems, my biggest gripe was not with the violent content (because what else would you expect down here), but the font they were written in. All of the massive, printed advertisements in Hell were written in the biggest, fattest, and most annoying font imaginable: Lobster.

I don't know about you, but I firmly believe Lobster font is attack on common decency and typefaces everywhere. Back when I was alive, sans-semi-Apocalypse, I could stand by Times New Roman. I could adapt to Arial. I might've even thrown down a Wingding or two on a quiet Friday night. But typing *every single advertisement* in Hell in Lobster font was an affront to the living and the dead alike—it was worse than Comic Sans. If this was the kind of minute torture I had to look forward to for the rest of my afterlife, Hell was truly going to be a place of pure misery.

We moved with purpose, a brisk ten-minute pace that was at times hard to keep up with. At one point, Cain slapped a hand on my shoulder and pulled me back a few paces behind Palls, who either didn't seem to notice or didn't need to care.

"Look, about what happened back in the human world. I screwed up, okay?" Cain told me. "Barnem was a tool and I kind of just jumped on the bandwagon. If you don't trust me—"

"We're good, Cain. It's fine." My reply stopped the ex-angel short.

"It's … *fine*? Darlin', I almost massacred your entire race."

"Let's chalk it up to poor career choices and move on." But I wasn't looking at her when I said this. "What do you know about him?"

Cain glanced over to Palls and shook her head. "Just that he's bad business. I always knew never to trust a Shade—no offense—but he's one I would be really careful with, especially in this city. There's a reason you have to walk around all covered up and he gets to strut around without anything hiding what he is. Let's just leave it at that." The angel then winked at me. "No worries, gorgeous. If he tries something, I'll slice his head off."

I could only see the bottom of her face as she brought her finger to her lips to keep that last bit between us.

Palls sighed and stopped short. "We're here."

Cain and I made the same tortured sound when, in unison, we spotted the place Palls had chosen for our private meeting.

"Out of all the places in Hell, you're making us go in *there*?" I asked. "I would rather be tortured to death by Mason while hearing him lecture me about rudely bleeding on him."

"It's the only place where folks will be too caught up in their own misery to pay us any mind," Palls explained. "If you have a better spot, then by all means."

Watching my two unlikely companions make off toward the establishment, I tugged the hood closer to my face and yelled after them. "Just so both of you know, so far, Hell really sucks."

"No, wait. Stop!" I pleaded, throwing my hands up. "There's way too much for me to understand. I don't get it. I don't get *any* of this."

Cain didn't pay me any mind. She had amassed four cups of water around her and was chugging each one down like it was her first gulp of liquid in centuries. Palls, on the other hand, crossed his arms and closed his eyes, as if his happy place was anywhere that didn't involve me. It probably was.

"Sure, Grey. What do you need me to explain?"

I flipped the menu over so he could see what I was looking at. "There are, like, twelve different names for pasta and all of them sound like venereal diseases. Not to mention it's all written in freakin' Lobster font. It's aggravating. I just want noodles with sauce. Someone point to noodles and sauce!"

The Olive Garden was packed, not an empty seat to be found. That's not saying much since even in my non-dead days I had yet to bear witness to an empty Olive Garden. My parents had taken me there once, more as an experience than as tried-and-true fans of what my mom dubbed "fast food served on a plate," and for the life of me I couldn't figure out why the place was so packed serving food that tasted like a soulless being from another planet had looked up the word "pasta" and started molesting noodles in an experiment to try and understand our species. All that aside, even in Hell there was a fifteen-minute wait for a booth.

There were, however, three things that informed me this Olive Garden was not, let's say, like the ones in my previous plane of existence.

The first thing, of course, was the other patrons. Besides Palls and me, there wasn't another human in sight. Cain looked human, but her death angel wings were a dead giveaway. Surrounding us in the other booths were giant insects with wings that rocked the low hanging lights when they buzzed, slugs with horned shells and eyes sprouting from every orifice, and multi-armed skeletons getting stuck in an endless loop of bro high fives and selfies.

The second unsettling thing about this restaurant was the cats, which were here in even higher numbers than the hotel. Hairballs and loose fur were everywhere, while the cats themselves sat in the light fixtures and lounged under seats. Some of the brave ones had no problem climbing right onto the tables to stare at patrons too busy conversing about how bitter the salad dressing was to care about a little extra cat dander in their food.

But the most unsettling thing about this place stopped just as Palls flagged him down at our table. The waiters in this Olive Garden not only sported the same uniform (white shirts, black vests, and pants) as they did in their undead counterpart, but they had tar-black skin and gray eyes. I had seen this look before. Petty had been turned into an undead puppet like this the first time she had died—not a zombie exactly, but pretty damn close. Looking at these husks walking around swelled a sizable knot in my throat.

So I'll admit it: the combination of the ghouls, the zombie waiters, and the slew of cats hanging around provided the perfect cocktail of a truly horrifying and rightfully adorable dining experience.

As if bored by it all, Palls let out a sound I could only describe as a toilet bowl trying to swallow two pounds of paper clips. In the new

lighting, I could really see this man as I hadn't before. Sitting a few feet from him still made me sick to my stomach, but I refused to give him the satisfaction of knowing this. Aside from the black pinstripe suit and the white wingtip shoes, not to mention the trench coat and fedora, he looked just as he had on the night he tried to kill me—still a broad human with square shoulders and hands the size of waffle irons. Every time he rattled his thick fingers against the table, my entire body shook.

Of course, the last time we met, his eyeball was missing and his teeth were all broken. This Palls looked younger and his skin was flawless. The punch I had recently gifted him back in the hotel hadn't even left a mark.

"Don't talk all at once, you two," I mumbled.

Cain set down her last cup of water and stretched her arms. "There's quite a bit to parse through, Grey."

"Fine, then," I replied. "Let's start with why there's an Olive Garden in Hell."

"People gotta make a living," Palls replied as the waiter leaned over and served us three more cups of ice water. Behind him, I spotted two cats biting and gnawing at the waiter's exposed ankle. The sound of tearing meat was nauseating.

As he walked away (his hungry fans literally nipping at his heels), a cat—a rather fat tabby—leapt up onto our table and began pawing at my saltshaker. After a few light taps, it knocked the whole thing over while no one said anything or moved to stop it. Its mission now complete, the cat jumped down to join its brethren snacking on our waiter.

"What's with the cats?" I asked, brooming the salt to the floor with my hand.

"Ever watched a cat just staring off into empty space?" Palls asked dryly. "Cats are incarnations of evil, Grey. They exist in both the living world and in the first three Circles of Hell. When you catch one acting odd or looking at shadows, those furry bastards are actually seeing the world down here." Palls pushed aside his plate and cutlery. "Look, I could sit here and answer all your grab-bag questions about the afterlife, Grey, or we can get to what matters. You don't trust me, right? Want to tell me how we can get over this hump?"

The truth was, I couldn't answer that question. I wasn't feeling like myself for some reason. I had gotten back my words and the ability to use my body, but there was still something hollow inside of me and it only seemed to be growing. Not wanting Palls to see me sweat, I replied in kind from behind my menu shield. "What can help us get over this? I would typically say it would take you dropping dead, but you kinda did already so… I got nothing."

"We don't have time—"

"You keep saying that," I interrupted, "'we don't have time.' But you haven't explained a single reason why I should believe you. Why are you doing this? What's your end-goal? And the million-dollar question: *who* got me into this dress?"

Palls snatched the menu from me. Instinctively, I stood up, scaring the four cats sleeping on the shelf above our heads and sending them into a mewing cluster. Palls remained seated but put his hands up as if he were a soldier surrendering. "We got off on the wrong foot."

"Because of *you*, my whole life imploded. Half of New York was destroyed. My apartment is gone. My parents are missing. That's not the wrong foot, Palls; it's a whole other fucking body. I mean, my life wasn't exactly something to write home about, I'll admit that. But I went from wondering when my next meal was going to come to constantly being attacked by demons and angels and cults and faux captains. The people I love nearly died. I nearly died!" The truth of those words struck me so hard that I sat back down. "I *did* die."

Palls put his hands down and closed his eyes. "You want to know how people get around in this city? Either by the train or Shadow Beast. Want to know what's the worst day of the week down here? Wednesday, because that's when the goblins hatch. Want to know what's the evilest entity in this entire city? The Post Office. I can sit here for a millennium answering all of your questions, but it won't matter. None of it will matter. We're wasting our time because you don't belong here. Your friend here promised to answer your questions, not me. I don't see the point. All I want to do—all I *need* to do—is bring you up one floor—just one floor—and you and me won't have to talk again. Ever."

"One floor? That doesn't mean anything to me. You might as well bend over and pull a map right out of your—"

"*We* are getting heated," Cain said, wedging her voice between ours. She slammed the last cup of water down and gestured for me to sit. "Grey has a point. She needs to know what this place is."

Palls eyes darted to her. "I advise against it."

"Well, then it's lucky she has me here. Don't forget, I'm an angel, honey. We don't listen to pieces of trash like you." Cain's harshness took me by surprise. Her face said it all: she hated Palls as much as I did. With the large man muted, Cain continued. "All right. So, let me try to make this easy enough for even a human to understand. Check this out."

The former angel took three cups and stacked each one on top of the other.

"There are Nine Circles of Hell." She pointed to each cup. "Right now, we are in what's called Ante-Hell which is only its first three Circles. You woke up in Circle Three, which is currently run by your friend, Mason. We are currently in the Second Circle"—she gestured around us, indicating the larger city— "also known as New Necro. I guess the good news is you're just a hop-skip-and-a-jump to the top Circle of Hell, Circle One: Limbo." She gestured over to Palls as if to say, *see?*

Stoic as ever, Palls stared straight ahead. "Someone hired me to get both you and your sister out of Hell. That's all you gotta know, so that's all I gotta say."

"Someone 'hired' you?" But I saw that Palls had shut down again. Flustered, I turned to Cain. "Why was Mason down there? What do you mean he 'runs the place?'"

Our waiter arrived, cat parade in tow, and deposited a fresh basket of breadsticks on our table.

Cain sighed. "Mason Scarborough allowed his soul to be swallowed by a Shade. Shades are not your run-of-the-mill demons. They are concentrations of pure evil created to plague mankind."

I nodded and avoiding reading too deeply into that. "Noted. Continue."

"Souls that have been clouded by their evils become Shade Wraiths when they die. That means their souls are eternally bound to Hell. Most people down here know these beings as Wardens. Since his death, Mason became the Warden of the Third Circle, The Hotel Gul. It's the place in Hell where consumers are tortured. They eat, they are eaten, and they wake up again. Every night. Until the end of eternity."

I raised my eyebrows and snuck a look at Palls, who angrily shoved a mashed breadstick into his mouth and started chewing as he blinked … very … slowly.

Cain and I looked at each other. We each grabbed a breadstick, too.

"You said Petty isn't down there, but she was at one point? Palls was telling the truth?"

Palls feigned a laugh. "Well, gee. Who woulda thought?"

"'Well, gee'? When were you born, Palls? The 1920s?"

"'23, actually." Palls kept chewing the same mouthful of bread. "Wanna know my shoe size too or did we pass the threshold of being 'best friends' already?"

Cain rapped her knuckles on the table, grabbing our attention like we were two dogs yapping at each other through a fence. After chewing on the bread for a while, the ex-angel said, "Ever since, you know, the almost-Apocalypse thing, I've been trying to get a job. I'll admit it didn't really pan out the way I wanted it to. Been working down there for only a few days, but I recognized Petty as soon as she got here. She was summoned up almost right away, though. Didn't get a second to talk to her."

Spotting the confusion on my face, Cain held up her hand. Petty had died way before I confronted that bastard Barnem in Saint Patrick's Cathedral.

"I know it's a hard thing to wrap your mortal mind around," the ex-angel explained. "You probably feel like you *just* died, but time doesn't work the same way down here as it does in your existence, Grey. Not in Heaven or in Hell. Take it from someone who was in that line of business for a *long* time. Petty might have died a while ago on your earth, but it takes a bit to process the soul. Paperwork, email chains…you name it. Business as usual in the afterlife."

I took a big bite of the breadstick and thought about my options.

Considering our history, Cain was probably the last person I should be trusting. She had manipulated me into thinking that D, my roommate, was out to kill me. She had been in cahoots with Barnem, the worst fucking Seraph I had ever met, and the mastermind behind the attempted destruction of humanity. But then there was also Palls, who I couldn't even stand being two feet from. How were we supposed to make this work?

Suddenly, all three of us, as if our sick had synchronized, spat the breadsticks from our mouths. Cain coughed hers out onto the floor, Palls caught his in a napkin, and I dumped mine into a cup.

"I'm pretty sure bread isn't supposed to taste like a human foot," Cain exclaimed.

Palls was pale. "Not sure if this tastes like crap because it's Hell or because it's part of their business model."

I looked down into my cup and pointed at the lump of mush. "Is it weird that it looks more edible now?"

Realization dawned on me. Watching the three of us wheeze and cough on appetizers that tasted like dough made in a janitor's mop bucket was a big, fat blazing sign; it was the universe trying to tell me something. Maybe it was saying that this ridiculously nonsensical group I had found myself part of was the only thing that made sense. Maybe the best company I could keep was a passive maniac and unemployed angel. I knew I shouldn't trust either of these people, but to be honest, what other choice did I have?

Besides, I hadn't been feeling well since waking up in this place—or, in the place I had woken up, or whatever. Something was off, and not in the whole "I'm dead" or "This is not my real body" kind of way. I felt emotionally stripped down. I couldn't get as angry or upset or even as salty as I wanted to. It felt like I was smashing myself up against a wall. Something was holding me back.

Because of this, I made up my mind.

"I have a few things I'd like to declare," I told Palls and Cain, rising to my feet. After quickly fixing my robes and nearly stepping on a cat lapping at the lump of breadstuff Cain had hocked onto the ground, I squared my shoulders and looked directly at the two people who had only served as major pains in my life.

"First thing, Olive Garden sucks and somehow makes Hell worse. Second, no one wants to explain how I got into this dress, but that's fine. I'm not going to hang onto that. Third…" This next part was extremely difficult to get out, but I took a deep breath and powered through it. "I'm here to find Petty. If she's up there, then let's get this show on the road. I mean, it's not like I can die again, right?"

This time, Cain and Palls exchanged glances and both yelled, "Check, please."

As we stepped out into New Necro once more, I could tell both of my guides were trying to ignore my question. So, naturally, I asked it again.

"So I can die? *Again*?"

Cain reached over and pinched my arm so hard I nearly fell over. Pointing to where I rubbed, she explained, "This existence is one without bones or blood, Grey. It runs on pain, pleasure, and fear—that's it. Simple. That's what all this is: an exercise in torture. You may not break a bone, but you'll feel it. You may not be breathing, but you sure as hell can feel strangled. You're even fitted with tears and the capacity to cry, probably as a way for them to get their rocks off, but point blank: you're a soul tethered to a vessel of punishment, Grey. If that body is destroyed, then so is your soul."

"But where does it go?"

"Nowhere. Doesn't go up. Doesn't go down. You die here, and then you vanish. We call it 'voiding out'." Hooking her arm into mine, she led me down the street. "Look, gorgeous. You got me here, okay? I'm walking you all the way to the train. A personal escort, free of charge. Nothing's going to happen with me here. And for all it's worth, Palls isn't a slouch either. For now, let's just walk."

In the open air of New Necro, I couldn't help but gawk again at its skyscrapers and packed streets. It reminded me so much of New York City that I questioned whether this was all some sort of wild nightmare. At the center of the city was a black skyscraper with no windows, just a black spire that stuck out of the ground like a thorn. This main building rose into the sky and vanished through the clouds. No other building in New Necro even came close to its height.

Palls pointed at the top of this landmark. "Guess where we gotta go."

I sighed and started following my guides down the street. "How do we get there?"

"We can go through the main building, but it's risky," Palls replied. "There's a train that workers use to get up to Limbo. We're going to ride it all the way to the top. All we have to worry about is getting across town without being seen. That's fourteen blocks of walking. Just keep your head down, your hood on, and your mouth shut."

Well, that proved to be next to impossible. Both Cain and Palls walked fast and between my smaller steps and the confinement of the robes, I quickly found myself falling behind. At one point I stumbled and completely lost sight of both of them. Poof—they were gone.

Looking around nervously, I crossed against the traffic. A slender creature with a triangular shaped head and black scales stuffed into a form-fitting suit stepped in front of me. With its yellow slits glowing like dying embers and a voice that was an avalanche of shattered glass, it wheezed out a, "Hi there, beautiful! Lemme ask you a question?"

Now, my typical response would be to threaten violence upon this creep's softer bits. But seeing as though Cain had told me to keep to myself (plus the fact that I couldn't find the gonads of a serpent even if I tried) I decided to listen to my guide. Keeping my hood closed, I tried skirting around him, but the scaled creep slithered between my legs and popped up in front of me.

"Hey, hey. Just a question, doll-face. Did it hurt when you fell from Heaven?" It laughed, showering the concrete at my feet with purple saliva. Then it added, "And by this, I'm asking if it caused you discomfort when your ethereal form was cast out of paradise and came crashing into this realm of absolute pain and desolation?"

Rubbing my temples, I shoved the bastard aside and kept walking, taking note that demon catcalls were the fucking worst.

I found Cain and Palls on the corner up ahead, looking for ways to

navigate around a mob of creatures. The large mass of blue, red, and green-scaled skin, or spiny hairs, or bounds of fur, seemed to be surrounding a singular figure standing on an overturned box. His entire body reminded me of a centipede, if all of its legs and joints were made of wood. He wore glasses and waved a phone around in one of his hands so the light shined on everyone.

At his wriggling feet, sprawled out on the sidewalk, lay the largest rat I had ever seen. It was almost five feet tall and was wearing what looked like a tattered crimson cloak. Motionless, this creature looked dead among the other freaks. "Look," the spiny preacher shouted, "Look! Look! See how this under-dweller was recently caught in this city. We must be protected from a revolt from below. And only one being can protect us. One being who has not abandoned us! He has not," it yelled to the gathered mob. "He lives and loves us all. He loves you and His love is the Way. Give yourself to Him."

I had heard this spiel before, but I never thought I would hear it in Hell of all places. I leaned into Cain to whisper, "A street sermon?"

Cain groaned. "Sure is. Except it's probably not the kind you're used to."

"He has not abandoned us," the creature continued, beads of sweat streaking across its rough hide. "We are all His children and He will always love us." He paused for dramatic effect as the crowd of demons grew restless. "Remember the tenets He has passed down: 'Do not kill, do not lust, do not covet…'" It stopped mid-sentence as one of its many arms picked up a water jug and brought it to its chapped lips. After a few hefty swigs, he finished by saying, "… in that order. Ensure murder comes as a result of coveting and lusting."

A few of the creatures nearby nodded and let out a soft, "Of course. What are we, animals?"

One of the mob, a large praying mantis-like demon, cast its bug eyes at me. I tugged my hood lower and tried to tuck it under my chin.

The insect reared on its hind legs and started crawling toward me at the exact same moment Palls created a clearing through the onlookers and pushed his way through. Using him as a blocker, I followed close by.

Suddenly, the crowd let out a series of *Ooo*s and *Ahh*s (and a few blood-curdling screams). As I cleared another demon gawker, I saw a large bird hovering over the preacher's head. With a wingspan of seven feet, and bring roughly five feet tall, its landing sent vibrations into the sidewalk.

Whispers spread throughout the group as the bird, whose shape I could now see was exactly like a crow's but made of burnt black flesh that dangled from its bones like melted rubber, parted its beak. An ear-piercing screech bowled out from its gullet, followed by a warbled voice that said:

"JUST HEARD THE MURDER RATE IN THE CITY IS AT AN ALL-TIME LOW! DISGRACEFUL. REMEMBER WHEN DISMEMBERMENT WAS AS COMMON AS A CUP OF COFFEE IN THIS TOWN? HASHTAG GOOD-NEIGHBORS-KILL-EACH-OTHER. HASHTAG NEW-NECRO-RUNS-ON-BLOOD-AND-TAXES."

Then, just like that, the bird dropped dead on the spot.

This seemed to stir the demons into a frenzy. They began thrashing about, swinging their tails, wailing into the night.

Rushing to get out, I realized I had lost sight of Palls and Cain in the fray—again. Still, I kept pushing through, trying my best to get to the end of the block.

"I saw someone strange just now. She was just here," a shaking voice shouted. I guessed it was the mantis from before. Several demons took flight. Others crouched on all fours and began sniffing the ground. The street evangelist could be heard yelling, "Our Lord wishes blood. Blood. *Blood*."

Just when I thought I was going to be torn apart by the mob of demons, they all simply stopped and started backing away. Palls stood at the center of the mob, holding his black burning fist in the air. All the demons—except the preacher—ran away instantly, like roaches when you pop on a light.

Lowering his hand, Palls snatched the preacher's phone from his hand, smashed it on the floor, and kept walking.

Cowering like a blubbering idiot, the wooden centipede curled itself around the pieces of its mobile. Cain and I stepped over it and followed Palls deeper into the city of demons.

We made it to the train without another dumpster fire of an incident. Something told me that the way the demons had reacted to him made me even more suspicious of who Gaffrey Palls truly was. I had so many questions, but as usual all that got put on hold when we arrived at our destination.

The first revelation was one of perspective. Standing amid the tall buildings had kept me from seeing too far out into the horizon. I guess I was just used to Manhattan—the way you can reach the end of the island and stare out into the water, spot Lady Liberty, look out at New York's ugly step-sibling who is only popular by vicinity (New Jersey).

Not in New Necro. Instead, I found myself staring at a massive rock wall. In fact, this brown jagged wall of twisting stones ran for thousands of miles in either direction and up into the sky. That was the true nature of New Necropolis—a city built in the belly of a cave.

We arrived at a small cut outbuilding with a single door made out of what appeared to be pure glass set into a gold frame. Standing just to the right of this was a wide stone pedestal with a fat beetle perched atop. It had a round blue bulbous head and black thorny legs. Its shell glowed from the inside.

As the three of us approached, the bug buzzed to life. Palls snapped his fingers and like some hellish magician, he produced a tiny black flame on his index finger. After passing it through the insect's backside, a soft beep let us know that the glass door beside was now unlocked. But just as I tried to push it open, the door locked itself again. The bug's shell opened and rather than wings, which I had expected, it revealed pages, as if it were a living book. The pages turned and turned, backward then forward, until stopping and falling open.

"G-g-grey." The book bug spoke with a clattering chatter. "G-g-grey. No admiss-ss-ssion."

"She's with me," Palls said with an air of authority.

"Grey has been s-s-summoned down. Lower fl-fl-floor."

"She's being transferred." Palls banged the bug once with his fist. Clearly confused, it flipped its pages, rocked back and forth. It dawned on me how much it would suck to get this far to reuniting with my sister only to have a dumb beetle guarding a door getting in my way. The thought should have made me angry, but again, these feelings wriggled like little more than dying fish in my chest. What the hell was wrong with me? Why couldn't I *feel* anything?

Finally, the door unlocked and opened for me.

Exhaling, I turned around only to be tackled-hugged by Cain. Not only did she bind her arms around me, but she encased me in her wings, too. "It was really great to see you, beautiful."

Shocked by the warmth of her body, I patted her back lightly and mumbled, "Sorry about the job," to see if she would let me go.

But she didn't. "Bah. I'm going to get drunk tonight. I'll find another job. No worries. I just feel great being able to help you. Say hi to your sis for me?"

I nodded and turned back to the door. Another feeling spread against my neck and collarbone, but I couldn't name it. It was prickly and smothered my legs as well. Was I going to miss her? Was I scared? What the hell was wrong with this wonky body they had stuffed my soul into? Was it defective?

The book bug read Palls' name aloud and gave him no grief getting through. I didn't like the idea of being alone with Palls. Even though he hadn't seemed even remotely as dangerous as when we first met, I still didn't trust the man. There were too many things left unsaid—too many secrets. The fact that he had some kind of sway down here made me doubly suspicious. And Mason using the words "authority" and "jurisdiction" just flat out made my skin crawl.

As Cain waved goodbye from behind the door, Palls and I walked down a ramp with long tracing lights. For this being Hell, the space was surprisingly clean and modern. No cramped spaces. No odors that reminded me of a violent armpit. I don't know what I'd had in mind when people mentioned Hell, but I guess it made sense that even this would be better than New York Transit.

The metal train car rattled into the station: red metal with what looked like teeth-marks crunching into the actual surface. The seats were grooved to house any and all manner of body and carcass types and

featured a high ceiling for those beasties over eleven feet. Tiny fanged harpies gossiped in an odd language as they dangled upside-down from the train's handlebars. A two-foot demon topped with six-foot horns swung its tiny hooved feet while clicking away at his small cellphone. What I had originally thought was the result of someone taking a steaming dump in one corner of the train car quietly unfolded a newspaper and started filling out the crossword puzzle.

I slid into a seat by the window. Even though there were two empty spots around me, Palls clutched the pole and remained standing as the train lurched into motion. Four warbled tones came over the PA and a voice completely devoid of life informed us that, "Next stop, Limbo."

A few minutes passed and, beyond the pane of glass, I watched as the train left the darkness of the tunnel. The black walls fell away, revealing the entirety of New Necropolis in all its twisted splendor.

The outlying buildings closest to the cave walls were smaller than those inland, with some of their architecture sitting as dilapidated slums. Of course, there were giant advertisements everywhere—on buildings, on buses, on cars. There were advertisements for effective noose management, an app whose catchphrase was "Swipe Right for Sodomy," and—funnily enough—roommate postings on Craigslist. Sometimes there were signs that promoted other signs. All in Lobster font. I wanted to gouge my eyes out (true story: there was an ad for that service, too).

At its greatest height, I could see right into the center of the city where all of the real estate—the buildings and shoddy houses—just stopped, giving way to a large hole that seemed to tunnel into absolute darkness. The mouth of the hole spanned at least ten blocks in every direction. The higher we traveled, the more I saw black pockets rising from the edges of this pit. At first, I took these to be clouds of smoke, but they quickly dispersed, moving like dense shadows as they spread into the city.

I jumped back as one of the oversized, fleshy crows buzzed by the window.

"A Screetch." Palls leaned forward to stare out of the window. "They come up from the Maw. That's what that hole is called, if you're wondering."

I watched as another flock surged up and descended amongst the buildings. We were pretty high up now and I could see clear across to the other side of New Necro. It seemed like every few minutes, there was a new army of Screetches plunging into the skyline.

"What are they doing?"

"They carry messages from below. Three guesses as to which evil so-and-so is behind them," Palls replied and then, as if noticing how close the two of us were standing, he pulled away. "How are you feeling?"

I was so shocked by the question I almost thought it had come from the stain at the other end of the car. "What?"

Palls sighed. I could tell he regretted opening his mouth. "Just ... how are you dealing with the emptiness?" When I just stared, he sucked in a deep breath. "You're feeling something inside of you right now and you can't put your finger on it. It's scratching at you, like a slow nail tracing your back. You can't get as angry as you like. You can't get upset the way you're used to. Something's a bit off, like you're riding shotgun in someone else's body."

"How..." Instinctively, I hugged the cloak tighter around me.

"I'm—" Palls' lips struggled to form the words in his mouth. He left me with, "It's what it feels like without a Shade in you. All of those emotions, the panic attacks, the night terrors leaping out at you from everywhere. Feeling like your skin is on fire all the time. The stares..." He rubbed the back of his neck. "This is what it feels like to be free. You'll get used to it after a while."

I stared at him but he refused to make eye contact with me. "Who are you really, Palls?"

The world outside the window was cut off as we entered another tunnel. The lights flickered to life in the train car, casting everything in weird fluorescent light.

"Doesn't matter," he answered shortly. "Your sister's waiting for you up top and we won't have to talk ever again."

The doors opened and four chimes rang as the deadpan voice informed us: "This stop is Limbo. Please watch your step."

FROM THE TRAIN, we walked up a steep walkway that led to a round doorway with white light pouring from its other side. We walked through and…well, I'm not sure how to describe my first impression of Limbo.

There were hundreds of tiny islands, their soil silver and shiny, floating in mid-air. Twisting rainbows served as bridges between each weightless isle. I heard thunder but not from any one space, it just seemed to echo and tumble from the air itself. At the epicenter, four suns spun, orbiting each other in a tight helix. Every time their radiuses came close to colliding, the world was filled with a dull *Waaaaa-Waaaaa* sound.

"Grey," Palls said, snapping me out of my trance. "Don't go that way. That's the weird part of town. We're going this way."

He turned and led me toward a staircase and doorway floating within the white space.

"Yeah sure," I replied, scratching my head, because there was absolutely nothing "weird" about this new direction.

Now, I'm about to say I was shocked by what I saw as I walked through this floating door. And I say this knowing full well that I've already seen some/lived through/died as a result of some pretty twisted shit already. But yeah, I stand by my point here.

Less because it was so weird and more because it was all too *familiar*.

I remembered the last time I was in the high-end Asian fusion/coffee house/bed and breakfast previously known as the Hotel California. The memory wasn't pleasant, mainly because it had been the moment I found out I was carrying a Shade inside of me.

Still, the place was just as I remembered. The Asian hostess from before greeted us with a smile and grabbed two crimson menus. "Table for two?"

"Just here for a meeting," Palls explained.

As if recognizing him, a shock rippled through the hostess' body. "Of course! I'm so sorry. Yes, your guest is here already. They are waiting for you. This way, please."

As we made our way through the dining area, I couldn't help but notice the patrons eating around us. They sat in booths, hunched over their plates, but none of the restaurant-goers had faces. Without noses, eyebrows, eyes, or mouths, their heads looked as if they had been scrubbed completely clean of any distinguishing features.

Standing beside every table was an angel eating from the patron's plate. After chewing for a few minutes, they would raise a finger and explain—to the best of their ability—how the food tasted.

"Pepperoni is bland, but the pasta is properly cooked," one angel advised. The blank-faced patron clapped his hands together in joy.

As we walked past the dining tables, past the ugly chandeliers and faceless patrons, I began to realize the thought of seeing Petty again was starting to make me nervous. I wasn't sure if this emotion had anything to do with what Palls had told me about dealing with my emotions post-demon infestation, but for once, I ran with it. I wanted to feel excited and nervous about seeing my sister again without feeling crushed by emotion. I wanted to feel happy and connected and scared, but I needed to find the right balance. These were emotions not chewed up and swallowed by anxiety, and I was just getting used to it.

Even with this in mind, I found it hard following obediently behind to the hostess when what I really wanted to do was bowl her over and run into the room where my sister was waiting. I had come all this way to see Petunia Grey again—my beautiful, brilliant, little dipshit of a sister.

I still remembered watching a demon consume her body. I remember carrying her lifeless corpse to the hospital.

That night, we had been torn from each other right when we were finally starting to reconnect. Like her body, I was still carrying the weight of those memories—and of her death—with me. I couldn't wait to tell her how sorry I was. I couldn't wait to get my family back. I didn't know what had happened to my mom and dad, but I was hoping this would be the beginning of me getting my life (er, afterlife) together.

Of course, Palls could have been setting me up for something, too. I was going by his word and Cain's confidence—two things that didn't exactly mean much in the grand scheme of things. But I was already in Hell. What did I have to lose?

When the receptionist reached the massive doors, I couldn't wait for her to open them. I shoulder-shoved her out of the way and threw all of my weight into opening them myself. At first, the doors didn't budge... but then they creaked. Then they shook. And then they slid open and I stumbled into the room.

The space was entirely as I remembered it: a long silver table with tall sloping chairs huddled around the edges. The high ceiling and almost blindingly white walls were the same. Of course, I didn't give a shit about the decor. What had my undivided attention was the figure standing on the farthest side of the table, dressed all in white, one arm propped up on the backrest of a chair.

But this person wasn't who I was expecting.

"D?"

He grinned. "Yo."

I can't tell you how I was able to recognize him so quickly. I don't remember ever seeing him wear a perfectly tailored white suit. Or have his black hair combed back and slick. Or smile. I had seen this guy transform from a blobby little creature to a young man my age that was—and I hesitate to use this phrase because he is a demon from Hell—oddly handsome. But I had never seen D, the Shade of the Apocalypse, smile.

The only real problem was that even though he was the D that I remembered; he was also more *demon* than I remembered him being. He had two curved horns sprouting from his head and he wore black nail polish. His mouth was even decorated with four very sharp fangs.

But there he was.

I felt like my entire chest had been folded into an accordion. My arms went numb. I was genuinely happy to see D, but he was *not* my dead sister—the sole reason I had come to Limbo in the first place. So you can't blame me for blurting out the first thing that came to mind.

"Where's Petty?"

D, the Shade who was coming around the table to greet me, stopped in his tracks. "Why would Petty be here? She was supposed to come up with you and Palls."

"Someone changed the plan on us," Palls chimed in as he entered the room behind me. "Kinda thought it was you."

"It wasn't," D replied, obviously miffed.

"They said she was called up here."

"She wasn't." As if his answer was only the second most important thing on his mind, D walked right up and threw a hug on me that caught me completely by surprise. It dawned on me—pressed against him—that the last time I'd seen him, I had been slowly slipping out of consciousness in his arms. His hug felt firm and, more importantly, genuine. If someone were to ask me how to describe this reunion hug, I would probably just make a weird duck sound (because I am totally good with the feelings).

"You all right, Grey?" he whispered in my ear.

I pushed away, shaking my head. *Was he always this tall?* "Petty?" I asked.

"Not sure what happened, but I promise we'll get this figured out. Right now, you need to come back with me."

I narrowed my eyes at his two pointed horns and the sharp fangs bulging out of his mouth. He truly looked like a full-fledged demon. A handsome one, but still creepy. His eyes even had rivets of red in them and he was definitely wearing guy-liner.

Laughing a bit to myself, I told him, "Why is everyone rushing me everywhere? You all act like you can't spare a minute or two. It's not the end of the world, D."

I said that, and it had the effect of sucking all of the air out of the room. D's eyes darted around like they were desperately asking for

someone—anyone—else to share their two cents in this conversation. When no one did, he cleared his throat. "So, about that. The last time you and I met, the last time I saw you alive...."

While D was preoccupied trying to assemble words into a sentence I could understand, the doors swung open and a chubby Asian man waddled his way in. He wore an aqua cumber bun beneath his baby blue blazer with matching pants. His hair didn't so much sit on his head as it worked like whip cream does to froth and decorate the top of his scalp. Flanking him were two female demons in slinky brown dresses. Each wore a satin lace veil, propped up by two tiny horns.

"G-G-G-GREY! There's my girl. There's my girl."

He whipped off his sunglasses and dotted a kiss on both of my cheeks. The only reason I didn't clock him in his big, fat face was because I felt like I knew him. I decided, at least for the moment, not to break his jaw until *after* remembering who the hell he was.

"Oh, look at us," he squealed when he saw D standing a few feet behind me. "Team Grey, back together again."

I tensed up. "You? The Smilie Cult guy?"

"Shuu," he said, placing a hand on his chest and bowing ever so slightly. "We never formally met, I realize. But yes, I heard you had arrived and *had* to come up. I had to come and say hello, pay my respects."

"That's great," I replied shooing Shuu away. "D, what were you about to say?"

"It's just that..." D winced as if the words in his mouth were stabbing into his tongue. Finally, he started with, "There's a lot to process."

"Why does everyone say that?"

"I'm sorry," Shuu cut in again. "I feel like I'm butting in on something important."

"You are. Speak up, D."

But Shuu wouldn't shut up. "So, I'm the Warden here in Limbo. Not a bad gig, huh? I provide some food service. Some music. All for the folks waiting for something to open up either above or below. Been slow recently but otherwise, business is great—it's *so* great. Having you and Palls here, Amanda, is like having a celebrity in our midst."

"Shuu. Why don't you go—"

"It's a shame I sent your sister down or this would be a real reunion of Team Grey."

The entire room went silent. Palls, D, me: we snapped our necks, all six of our eyes zeroing in on Shuu.

"My sister? Petty was here?"

Shocked by our reaction, Shuu backed away. "Well, yes. I-I just sent her down. N-not a minute ago."

"*Down*?" Palls stepped right in front of the small Asian fusion/coffee house/bed and breakfast owner of Limbo. "Down where?"

Sensing an impending ass whooping, Shuu ducked behind his escorts. The two ladies set out their hands and long claws emerged from their fingers like swords. Their bodies began puffing up and hundreds of needles sprouted out of their backs so that they resembled fashionable porcupines.

Seeing Palls wasn't backing down, the small owner yelled and held his hands up. "A Screech came just a few minutes ago. It said Petunia Grey was to be sent down immediately. So that's what I did. C'mon. It was a Screech, Palls. You know who's the only guy who uses Screeches."

I pushed by Palls, through the pointy women, and got right up in Shuu's sweaty face so I could bite off each word right in his mug. "Down. Where?"

The man gulped.

"All the way down. The lowest. She was called down to the bottom floor—the Ninth Circle of Hell."

I DROPPED MYSELF in a chair and banged my head down on the table so hard it made a hollow sound (the table, not my head).

Following the news of Petty's fate, Palls grumbled, "Let's give these two some breathing room." Before Shuu could disagree, Palls picked him up by the neck like a naughty cat and carried him out, his associates following closely behind. D and Palls met eyes as the doors closed, but neither said a word.

D took a seat next to me and I turned my head slightly to face him. Blowing aside my hair for an unobstructed view of my former roommate, I couldn't help but notice how freakish he looked up close.

"What's with..." I made circles around my head in regards to his demon-regalia.

"Oh," D exclaimed. As if just realizing, he reached up and tore off one of his horns and placed it on the table in front of me, revealing its papier-mâché lining. He then flicked out his red contact and spit out his fangs and placed both of these down on the table.

"You're wearing a costume?"

"Back in the world of the living, it's Halloween, Grey."

"You're dressed as a demon."

"Yeah?"

"But you *are a* demon. Who taught you Halloween rules, buddy? The whole point is that you're supposed to go as something completely different from what you are."

D's eyes opened wide. "You still rant when you're overstressed, I see." And then he laughed. I don't think I'd ever heard D laugh. It was large and blew from his mouth so effortlessly that I forgot what we were talking about.

When he was through, we sat in silence for a bit. I didn't know where to start, but thank goodness, he already had something in mind. "I don't mean to put this all on your plate, Grey. I know you're dealing with a lot."

"Sorry to break it to you, but my plate's been full ever since kindergarten," I replied with a smirk. "Don't even know what an empty plate feels like so just … bring it on."

D tapped his finger on the table. "A lot's changed since you've been gone." It was painfully obvious what he was walking around the edges of, so I just asked. Time to rip off the Band-Aid. "How long has it been, D? When was the last time I saw you?"

D hung his head. "Two years ago."

I wanted to ask him to repeat himself. Had I heard wrong? Two *years*? Did he mean two weeks? Two hours?

"Trust me. I understand how this gets knotted up in your head. New York is still New York. A bit weirder since you left, but the coffee's still bitter and the rent is still high."

I buried my head in my hands. "Good to hear."

I could tell by his sigh that D had more to tell me. "Grey, your father isn't doing too good."

Even though I felt emotionally spent, this sent a charge through me. "What are you talking about? My mom and dad?"

"It took me some time to find them after you left, but I did. That kid from the Vatican was taking care of them. Your mother cried and cried when I told them about you and Petty. Your father … your father wasn't the same after that." D took off his other horn and played with it.

Choking back tears, I told him, "I need to see him before …"

D nodded. "That's why I came to get you and Petty out of here. I can manage it, busting you out into the real world. It wouldn't be permanent, you understand? But at least you would be able to see him. You two were supposed to come with me."

Shuu's words echoed in my head.

"What does he mean by the bottom floor? Who summoned Petunia down there?"

D, visibly uncomfortable, stood up and started pacing. "The bottom floor of Hell: reserved for the truly damned and ... one other being. He hasn't been seen or heard from directly in centuries, well, not until recently. Those Screeches are his messengers."

I envisioned the black fleshy birds skimming along the city rooftops. The dark voice spilling out of their beaks.

"The Devil took my sister," I said slowly.

For whatever reason, D took my words the same way someone would if they'd eaten half a plate of rusted screws. He comically clutched at his stomach.

"Wow. I'm getting this really weird feeling for some reason. It's weird but oh-so-familiar. Kinda reminds me of the large pit that used to grow in my stomach every time you were about to propose a plan that was absolutely terri—"

"I'm going down to get Petty!"

D snapped his fingers. "There it is!"

"I'm not leaving her behind," I explained nicely, and by this, I meant I was waiting to punch him in the throat if he gave me lip about it.

Desperate to find a solid point to grasp onto, D tried to reason with me. "What about your father, Grey?"

I took a deep breath and rose from my chair. "You wanted to bring both of us to see him. *Both*, me and Petty. If I can't keep Petty safe, then I don't deserve to face Dad again. I ... I think he would understand that. I hope he would."

D put all of his weight into his knuckles and leaned into the table. Looking me directly in the eyes, he started, "Fine. But just so you know, we're not talking about a casual afterlife romp here. Don't forget that once you leave Limbo, you'll have to navigate an entire city of demons. Then, you have to deal with the hotel sitting in the very throat of hell whose owner, for your information, wants nothing more than to torture your soul for eternity. And all that's a cakewalk considering what you're

up against in the lower Circles. The Fourth Circle is the stomach that digests the greedy and power hungry, while the River Styx waits to drown the rage-filled souls in the Fifth Circle. I can't tell you what's below that, but I'm guessing more torture, more pain, and more desecration of the human mind. And all of this excludes the fact that the absolute embodiment of pure evil, the awakener of lies and sin, stirs at the bottom of this chasm. He's the one you'll have to face to get your sister's soul back."

I thought about it for a second. "Okay."

D pinched his nose and yelled, "Cool! So, just for the record, Grey?"

"Yup?"

"Did any of that register at all? The stomach digestion? Torturing your soul? Etcetera, Etcetera."

"Heard it all."

"And did any of it scare the living shit out of you?"

"All of it," I replied with a hearty thumbs-up, "but if the Devil has my sister, then I guess I'll just have to go get her back."

It was such a simple response D had no counter for it, so he simply shrugged. As if on cue, Palls walked in. The large man took one look at D and then at me and immediately threw his head back as he rubbed his face.

"You're going down to get her, aren't you?" D nodded slowly and I smiled as confidently as I could manage. Palls pointed a finger at me. "This isn't going to be some cozy picnic, Grey. The moment you get out of Limbo, you'll have all of New Necro to contend with. After that, it's—"

But D waved him off. "Save your breath, Palls. I explained it all already."

"Really? And she still wants to go?" He looked at me sternly, as if he were posing for his Mount Rushmore carving. Then Palls replied, "Fine. I'm going, too. I'll be waiting up front."

Then he walked out. Just like that.

I was turning to D to ask what the hell that was about, but the Shade looked as if he had something to say. I didn't need to be a mind reader to know what it was.

"But listen—"

"No."

"He knows the city, Grey. Have you seen New Necro? I'll be the first to admit that you kick a whole lot of ass on your own, Amanda Grey. But this isn't Queens. This isn't even Earth. That city is just *one* of Nine Circles of Hell. Without help, you'll void out long before you get to Petty. And then what's all of this for?"

I couldn't believe D. Having to deal with him partnering up with this madman to pull me out of Hell was one thing, but trusting Palls enough to join us as we dove through Nine Circles of Hell just to save Petty's soul was a bridge too freaking far.

"Don't give me that look," D said, scolding me even though he wasn't facing me to know what look I was tossing him.

"I have many looks, D. Many! Right now I can't decide between 'I'm so screwed' and 'Is it too soon to uppercut my ex-roommate'." I ran my fingers down my face, trying to smooth out the unpleasant thoughts. "Fine. Whatever. My life has been filled with terrible ideas. What's one more?"

With that, D nodded and started making his way toward the door. That's when the realization hit: he wasn't coming with me.

I'd never thought I was going to see D again, let alone think I would feel upset he was leaving. I still had memories of him back when he was a little black carnivorous blob—back when I had no idea whether he was harmless or the Antichrist. I guess he turned out just to be my friend.

Looking back over his shoulder, D read the strain on my face and sighed.

"Just lay low and get through the first Four Circles, Grey. I'll be waiting on the Fifth to take you the rest of the way down. I promise."

"Wait," I shouted, and D froze by the door.

He turned to me slowly.

"Why are you doing this? Why do you want to bring me back?"

D nodded as if this question was one he'd already prepared an answer for. He pushed the doors open and, just before sliding his body through, he winked and responded:

"Because the world just isn't the same without you, Amanda Grey."

Palls sat across from me on the train ride back in his now-typical pose: arms crossed, eyes closed, and aura of total irritation. I watched the city of New Necro stream into view again as we slowly made our way down from Limbo. I felt so small compared to the city in front of me, especially knowing this was only the Second Circle of an entire afterlife and there was still a long way down to go.

"Why are some of these stores ... actual stores?" I asked as an attempt at small talk.

"They're not *the* stores you know," Palls grumbled, "they're just marketed that way. For instance, you see that place down there? That place is called 'Rite Aid.' We call it that because they poison you when you first walk in and force you to find the right antidote hidden among the two million choices."

"I see. What about that one? It says 'H&M'?"

"Stands for 'Hornets & Mice.' And before you ask, yes you get to hold the creatures but no, not in your hands."

Spotting a third one, I added, "Hmm. What do they do to you in the one called 'Ikea'?"

Palls' face went as still as a grave. "That's just an Ikea."

"Oh." It made sense.

When we were close to pulling into the station, Palls slapped both of his palms on his knees, a sign he had finally decided to toss some real thoughts my way. "All right, Grey. If this is going to be anywhere near successful, you'll need to know a thing or two about what's going on—not only in the city, but in all of Hell."

I sat up straight. "Let's do it."

"The first thing is about the guy in charge. If you're really going down, just know the Dark Lord doesn't normally take guests. But ever since your little scuffle with the Shades, he's gotten more ... proactive. And now we have those things." He pointed to a large pocket of Screeches spewing up from the Maw. "He sends his messengers around, causes chaos. Loves it. Feeds off it. For some reason, also makes hashtags for it. Either way, he has your sister and now you're going down to meet him face-to-face. Sounds pretty damn stupid to me, but that's only if you're asking my opinion."

I thrust a single finger in the air, and it didn't take a genius to guess which one. "I'm not."

Palls continued.

"Second thing you need to know is that you can't go around punching things when we get inside New Necro. The folks in the city aren't demons—at least not yet. Humans are housed in the other Circles, but regardless of how the folks of New Necro look, they're neutral, which means they can be pushed to the light or the dark. They can be monsters, but that's only if there's no one to keep them in check."

Seeing the sternness on his face told me all I needed to know. "Is that what you do, Palls? Like Mason? Like Shuu? You keep them 'in check.' You're the Warden of this Circle of Hell, aren't you?"

Even though I had figured it out all on my own and kind of thought it was impressive, Gaffrey Palls wore the cold expression of an Easter Island decoration. Looking at what he wore—the trench coat, the hat, the sloppy shirt and tie—he looked like a slovenly detective right out of the pages of a pulp story.

"It's not an easy gig, keeping this city running. Six hundred and sixty-six blocks, four boroughs, and over a million demons trying to find their way. We got a small crew down here that keeps the peace, folks that help me out. But it still takes a lot out of you. Just when you think you've seen it all, this city still finds a way to surprise you." Palls stared out at the tall skyscrapers, looking weirdly wistful.

Out among the buildings, I spotted a massive creature bounding through the streets. Standing at about eight stories tall, a black wolf stood like a shadow against the glass buildings. Bright yellow windows ran alongside its body, neck to tail. I could just make out the silhouettes of passengers inside this bounding creature. In other parts of the city, two other wolves stalked their sides of the sprawling city.

"Are those the shadow beasts?"

"Yup. The Cerberus Line can get you anywhere you need to go at half the cost of a cab and in a short time." Palls took one look at me and let out a long exhale. "You know, you're something else. After seeing all this, after realizing what you're up against, you're not scared. Not even a little bit?"

Giving my back to the window, I stared at the last person in the world I thought I would ever see again, let alone speak to—let alone partner with. I flashed him my cheesiest smile and declared, "Oh, no. I'm scared shitless. It's just… I'm kind of used to dealing with stress by punching or yelling at it until it dies."

Palls rubbed his chin. "I see."

"And what about you? This isn't going to work if I don't know why you're tagging along, Palls."

The tall man shifted to the other side of the pole and flipped his hat off. "If you must know, I'm only going with you because the Wardens from the circles down below have gone missing."

"Wardens?" I shook my head. "Like Mason? Like you? Even Mr. Smiley up in Limbo? The guy who I caught feeding off of people in a cult? You're out to save them?"

Palls huffed. "We're still people, Grey. So what if we're not going to be winning any humanitarian awards any time soon. Like it or not, Wardens like Mason and Shuu, and yes even me, we keep the order, Grey. And if that's going to stand, I need to see what's happening down there for myself." Palls fixed his coat. "This isn't about anything else but my job, so we don't have to be friends after. You go your way and I go mine."

I chuckled. "Your job, huh? And here I thought you were just here to babysit me and make sure I didn't touch anything."

Palls plopped his hat back on his head and tipped the brim. "Sorry, Grey. Job's more important." The train jerked as it lurched to stop. Palls walked to the door and, as it slid open, he added, "But seriously. Don't touch anything."

I sucked my teeth as he exited. "It's just a city full of demons, Palls. Who says I need your help?"

Palls made it very clear we needed to find Cain—now.

"She'll know how to get us as far as the Fourth Circle," he explained, adding very little other information.

The moment we arrived at street level, Palls pulled us over to a large metal basin with a receiver and keypad attached. I couldn't believe what I was seeing. It took an entire minute of gasping and blubbering for me to get any words out—a new record.

"Holy. Shit. Is that a pay phone?" I slapped my forehead. "Back in New York, you've got a higher chance of meeting one of the subway mole people than find a working pay phone. You don't have a cellphone?"

Palls tucked the receiver between his shoulder and ear. "Just call me old fashioned." He tapped a number into the pad, and then produced a pen and slip of paper from his coat pocket. While I didn't get all of his conversation, I did catch the phrase "Fallen Registry" and Palls mumbled an address as he jotted it down. A minute later, he slammed the receiver down and folded up the paper, returning it to his breast pocket. Then, without so much as a how-do-you-do, we started walking again.

Making our way around New Necro was a mixture of a surreal dream and fucked up nightmare. Even though this place looked like my city—right down to its concrete blocks and traffic lights. But then there were the ten-foot spiders, and the rock golems, and the terrible Lobster font—more than once, I felt overwhelmed by it all. I opted to go back into hiding under the hood as I kept my feet moving.

"Where we headed?"

Palls tucked his hands in his coat pocket. "Cain's apartment. She lives in a walk-up ten blocks from here. Just keep moving."

More than one demon recognized Palls during our walk. One bird-like creature wearing a yellow turtleneck and flip-flops even walked up to him and began to protest, pointing with its wing for emphasis. It seemed to be shouting for Palls to follow him, but the man waved the bird-thing away. Apparently, the Warden was off the clock.

We only stopped once, and this was because a Screetch had landed nearby and collected a cluster of demons around it. After spotting the mob, we took the long way around, cutting down a side street to a block of small residentials. The sidewalk slabs were uneven. Garbage was strewn about. The streets sported potholes so large, I witnessed a cab fall into one and never come back out.

It made me miss my old neighborhood even more. Being homesick is a weird thing.

The standout, and what I was quickly distracted by, was that one of the buildings was on fire. I'm talking four or five alarms, roaring. All of the windows were open and large flames poured out, lighting up the entire block. Oddly enough, within the crackling flames, I caught a few dashes of playful laughter and screams of unbridled passion.

Palls groaned. "It's just wisps. One second." He walked up to the front door and banged on it, shouting, "Warden, here! You want to keep it down before you set the whole damn block on fire?"

The inferno immediately quelled to a low sizzle and I could see inside one of the windows. Beings of pure fire—male, female, and everything in between—strutted around, naked, their muscular frames revealing yellow and red tongues of flame that licked every inch of their fiery flesh. When their bodies collided, a mini-explosion would form and spread around the room, with more and more of its residents groaning in pleasure.

Palls banged just as the flames started getting higher again. "If I have to come back with a fire extinguisher to put your flaming privates out..."

The flames dropped again and stayed that way. Satisfied, Palls and I continued on.

Palls made us stop at the next building over, a six-story brown-bricked monstrosity with huge glowing windows. As he rung the buzzer for 6A, I glanced over at the neighboring building. Five skeletal corpses were strewn about the front steps. I thanked the gods we had found the building we needed.

Plucking the pad from his jacket pocket, Palls gave his writing a once over and squinted up at the window. The panes were closed and all was dark. Muttering under his breath, he looked around.

I stood off to the side to let a couple of crab-like creatures walk by. "Problem, Palls?"

"This address is what's listed on the registry, but it's wrong."

"Registry?"

"The Fallen Star Registry. City makes fallen angels register for working papers, but nine times out of ten, Fallen give fake addresses to stay off the books. Just stay here for a sec."

Walking over to the next building, Palls stopped among the skeletons.

"How's everything, gentlemen?"

"All good, Warden," replied one of the skeletons in a light and airy voice.

"I'm looking for a Fallen Star. Female-looking, blonde. New to the block, probably. Got one of those in this neighborhood?"

The skeletons didn't respond right away. "We don't want no trouble," another replied.

Palls stooped down beside the one that had spoken. "That's … that's really good. Funny, I don't want trouble either. Who says civility doesn't exist in a city of demons?" Palls faked a smile that was horrible to look at. "I mean, I could have taken your head and punted it down the street when you didn't answer my question the first time. But I didn't, right? That was *really* civil of me."

The skeleton glanced to his fellows who seemed now to be truly dead.

"Uh," it chattered, "S-s-she's on the fourth floor of this building. But she stepped out. I-I-I can buzz you in and you can wait inside."

Palls stopped smiling and walked away as the skeleton shouted up to an open window on the second floor. A skull popped out and, in a female voice, asked what he wanted.

"O-o-open up for the Warden."

Palls stared up and the skeleton ducked inside, resulting in the door buzzer going off. Palls held it open with one hand and gestured for me to get in quickly.

Wanting to get off the street, I entered.

The main floor of this building was a long hallway of black and white tiles and a single elevator. Just inside the elevator's doors stood an elderly demon, holding groceries and pressing the hold button to stay the doors. She wore a knitted sweater and a gray skirt with pantyhose rolled to her ankles. Her purple skin was wrinkled like a worn paper bag and two little horns popped out of the bundle of white hair she had tied into a neat bun.

"Hold that door," I shouted.

The old demon lady waved for me to hurry. Out of habit, I started jogging to the elevator, but Palls slid in front of me.

"What's your—"

"The buildings on this block are pretty old. That means they're all walk-ups." Palls gestured over to a long winding staircase and then stared at the old demon woman in the elevator. "You really are a steaming pile of garbage, aren't you?"

I took a step toward him. "Uh, Palls?"

But he shot out his arm for me to keep my distance. "Stay out of this."

The elderly demon didn't move or speak. In fact, she didn't seem to be looking at us at all. Tracking her sightline, she was still staring at the front door behind us, waving softly to no one in particular.

"So, it's going to be the hard way, eh? All right." Palls walked in, grabbed the little woman by the neck, and dragged her out into the hallway.

Thinking Palls had finally lost his mind, I jumped on his back. I mean, beating up an old lady—even an old demon lady—was too far outside of my comfort zone to just watch it go down. Unfortunately, there wasn't much I could do as the large man wore me like a cheap book bag.

Right before my eyes, the little old lady morphed into what looked like a giant gray slug. Covered in thick mucus, it tried to wriggle free, but Palls bound his arms around it and held on. The slimy trail of its body seemed to be rooted into the floor of the elevator.

Suddenly, the sign where the floors were posted on the lift turned inward and two yellow eyeballs sprouted from it. The lights inside the

small space flickered off and on, and an awful wail belched out as teeth sprouted from the ceiling and floor.

What I had thought was an elevator was actually the mouth of a waiting demon.

Palls grabbed its slimy tongue with both hands.

"Mimicking without a license?"

"Kwaaaaa- waaaaa-waaaa," the large demon cried. "Weeeee-kawwww-weeee!"

"I'm sorry, I didn't catch that. Maybe I should tear this stupid thing out of your mouth and then ask you to speak up. How's that sound?"

Tears poured out of the dangling eyeballs.

Turning his head slightly, Palls addressed me. "Hey, Grey. While we have this guy here, we should ask for his opinion." Then, with me still on his back and while wrestling a tongue the size of a king-sized bed, Palls started speaking to it. "You see, Grey and I were having this argument. Well, let's call it more of a spirited disagreement. She says she doesn't need my help getting around New Necro. I disagree. I think she's just asking to get torn open, diced to pieces, or *eaten*. What do you think? You think I'm overreacting?"

The demon elevator looked at me. Its eyeballs were turning red and shaking under the strain. It was trying to say something. Spittle flew from the open mouth by the buckets and splashed out into the hallway.

Palls nodded. "See? I knew I wasn't in the wrong here."

Bracing himself, Palls pulled with all his might. I heard the rip of tissue as the demon screamed. At the last moment, the man let go, causing us to both fall on the floor as the tongue snapped back into the demon's mouth.

The creature tumbled down the shaft and vanished, leaving nothing but a thick trail of saliva and a vacant hole in the ground. I could hear it sobbing as it went. I knew it almost ate me, but it was still a little hard to listen to it cry.

Palls got up and shook the grossness off, then he then picked up his hat and wrung it out. Fixing his black hair, he turned to me and offered me his hand.

After pulling me to my feet, Gaffrey Palls plopped the hat back on his head and then pointed to the staircase, sarcastically adding, "After you."

"We don't have a key," I said, when we found the door to Cain's apartment locked.

"I got one right here."

Palls set his shoulder into the side of the apartment door and knocked the whole damn thing off the hinges. After watching him dust off the splinters from his jacket, I stepped over the carnage to survey the room.

The place was an absolute pigsty. Honestly, I thought *I* was messy—Cain needed a blowtorch, or maybe a couple of wisps to have an orgy in there, to get this place anything close to tidy. There were beer cans everywhere, clothes piled into large mounds, broken furniture... Despite the fact that a single window was sitting wide open, the place still smelled like vinegar soaked foot fungus which may or may not have come from the cluster of what I *hoped* were empty pickle jars lined along the edges of the walls.

When we turned on the only light, a lamp with a broken neck, four cats glared up from their curled balls. Considering how vain Cain came across as, I would never have believed this was her apartment. There was no sign of a bed, bathroom, or kitchen—no sign that she gave a damn whatsoever. Her apartment reminded me more a city dump than a place of residence.

"Is this really where Cain lives?"

"She lives like a slob. All Fallen do." Palls lifted up a bag and tossed it aside. "What was your friend's profession before all of this again?"

"Angel of Death."

"Makes sense." Palls tore open a white garbage bag filled with clothes, spilling its contents out onto the floor. "She's used to collecting things. So much so it's now a tick. Most Fallen Stars develop coping mechanisms when they've been cast out of Paradise. Your friend is a hoarder. Here's something."

He tossed me a black shirt and a pair ripped blue jeans.

"What's this for?"

"It's so I don't have to keep hearing your mouth about your dress. You can get dressed back there. I won't peek."

I walked behind a large pile of newspapers, paying close attention to where Palls was standing at all times. As if to settle my nerves, the man made his way to the open window and kept talking so the silence didn't turn awkward. "Hopefully she has a way of getting us to the lower Circles that doesn't include facing Mason again. The city streets get clear every few hours, so we should move out then."

The shirt fit okay. I had to roll the sleeves up, but it was comfortable. The jeans had a good feel for them but needed a belt. I found one in a pile and, thankfully, unearthed some black sneakers my size from beneath a stash hidden under a holey blanket. I pulled one of the shoelaces out of a stray pair of shoes and used it to tie up my hair into a messy but perfectly functional ponytail.

"You know, you talk like a cop sometimes."

Palls chuckled. "That's because I used to be one."

I stopped short. "Woah. What? You're fucking with me."

"I'm not." Palls bent out to check the street. "Don't forget we were all human before Hell came into our lives, Grey. Just like you. Your friend Shuu—from Limbo? He ran his own beauty salon before his life got the Shade treatment. The Warden of the Fourth Circle had her own nanny business—in Sweden, I think."

I didn't want to tell Palls how much of a shock this was. When you've dealt with evil demons and apocalyptic events as much as I have, you forget people had lives behind the chaos—that they had friends and family. Hell, some even had—have—loved ones.

I quickly changed topics. "Do you think we should have come into her apartment like this?"

"Huh?"

"I'm just asking whether Cain would think she was getting robbed or something."

Palls thought for a minute. "Do you really think—"

He never got to finish that thought as shadow flew through the window, tackling him to the floor. The figure spread its wings and each plume seemed like a collection of razor-sharp daggers. Its face glowed in the darkness; its eyes and mouth burning white-hot embers.

I backed away and tripped on a rusted stack of stolen highway signs, sending the metal slabs clattering to the floor.

The figure turned and, seeing who I was, Cain flipped her hair and winked, causing the fearsome figure to melt away instantly. "Oh hi, Grey!"

"Hey, Cain." I pointed to the man still pinned beneath her foot. "That's Palls you got down there."

Cain looked down and back to me. "So it is." She looked around the apartment. "So where's your sis, Grey? Is Petty here?" She seemed excited. Even her wings perked up.

"Uh. A funny thing happened in Limbo, Cain."

The angel cocked her head to the side. "How funny?"

AFTER LISTENING TO what we had to say, Cain immediately told us, "You do know this is the worst freakin' plan I've ever heard in my life, right? And I'm an immortal being so that means a lot coming from me. I was around when God planted the Tree of Knowledge. And all of us were like, 'Uh. This seems kind of screwed up. You sure you shouldn't, like, not plant that here?' And He totally didn't say anything to us. He just giggled to Himself all *tee-hee*. Yeah, God giggles. What can I say? It was odd to me, too."

"She's still talking," I whispered to Palls, who wasn't listening. Still salty about being pinned beneath the former angel's foot, Palls seemed to have drowned Cain's rambling out.

As soon as she had heard our plan, Cain proceeded to have a meltdown. I'd only known a few angels, but I realized at that moment most angels must be like this: complainers. Barnem had been the absolute king of bitching. It seemed Cain wasn't far behind in line for the throne.

Unfortunately, thinking of that asshole brought up a burning question in my mind

"Is Barnem in Hell? *Please* tell me that scumbag ended up here."

Cain curled her arm around my neck. "Did he ever, and was he *livid* about it. First, he ended up in Hotel Gul because, obviously, he was tainted by the Shades. Then he asked to speak to management. Cross had him taken away and he's probably being tortured as we speak."

I exhaled. "At least something's going right."

"I really want to help, Grey. I really do. But this is a suicide mission. Rumor has it no one has been to see the Dark Lord in ages. He is the Big Boss, Grey—the Ultimate Evil. What's your plan for getting Petty out of there? You're going to sass your way out?"

I tapped my chin. "Would that work?"

"No."

"Then I'll play it by ear. Look, I don't have a plan, but maybe that's for the best."

Frustrated, Palls butted his way into the conversation. "If you really need to know, it was my idea to get you to go with us."

Cain rewarded this with a long slow-clap. "Oh, joy of joys. Thanks, buddy."

"We're headed down to the Fourth Circle. All we need is help getting there." Palls seemed to be choosing his next words carefully. "When was the last time you were down there, Cain? Must be hard being the only Fallen Star on the block."

Whatever this meant—and I had absolutely no idea—provoked the angle like nothing I could have anticipated. Slowly, she stood up and began stretching her neck. Stepping right up to Palls' face, Cain sneered, licking her lips in a way that sent a shiver down *my* spine and it wasn't even me she was talking to.

"You realize I don't care if you're a Warden or not. You call me that again and I'll cut you into tiny pieces."

Palls managed to look bored by it all.

The entire room was on edge. Even the cats in the apartment were up, tails in the air, hissing.

It was my turn to get in between the two. Clearing my throat, I said, "If we have to go to the Fourth Circle, I could really use your help, Cain."

Eyes still locked on the man in front of her, Cain replied, "Yeah, well. You're in luck then, beautiful. Just so happens that I'm due for a visit down there. I don't mind keeping *you* company. Just let me change."

Cain took a step back and took her shirt off, revealing her smooth skin and toned body. The only blemish I saw was a small bandage around her collarbone. Still red and puckering, the wound underneath it looked fresh.

Cain took her time walking topless around the apartment. Palls let us know he'd wait downstairs, though he was clear that his exit was not in a "I'm modest and don't want to make you feel uncomfortable" kind of way and more like "You're the least attractive creature on the planet and I'd rather feed my privates to a wood chipper."

Fishing through a pile of laundry, Cain selected a black crop-top shirt from the pile and slipped it on. Spotting me with my new clothes, she nodded in approval. She popped up a finger and went hunting for something. Then she handed me two brown boots and added, "To go with your jeans. How do they feel?"

For my first pair ever, the boots actually felt better than the sneakers. They also made me feel taller. Not as tall as Cain, all six feet of her, but I had to admit it wasn't a bad view from the extra inches.

"I didn't mean to force you into this."

"Oh, please," Cain snickered, sliding into a brown leather jacket. "I was only giving shit to his high-and-mightiness because Palls deserves it. Truthfully, I want to help. For you or your sister? Anything, Grey. Not to mention I've put off heading down for long enough."

"What do you have to do in the Fourth Circle, anyway?"

Cain stopped short. She spun around and touched her palm to one of my cheeks. "Can't sat it's as honorable as going to save my sister. No need to worry about it. You can count on me. I'll get you there in one piece." Pausing to correct herself, she added, "On second thought, let's just drop the 'one piece' part. I'll get *you* there. Let's not make promises we can't keep."

She tapped me on the shoulder and laughed as she exited the apartment.

Stunned for a few moments, I chased after her yelling, "No, let's. Let's make promises, Cain. I'm down for amending our friendship to include any and all promises of non-dismemberment."

Palls made sure to keep us off the main streets. Warden or not, he was definitely not interested in letting anyone know I was human. Taking this as sound advice, I kept my mouth shut and walked close, trying to be as inconspicuous as possible. As a unit, we weaved in and out of the city without too many bulging eyes (and twisting pincers and glancing suckers) on us for too long. This sometimes meant we had to veer into dark alleyways to avoid the city lights, which also meant walking past the shadiest of creatures lurking about. In one small parking lot, a fat spider draped in a fur jacket dropped from a streetlight and tried to scalp me tickets to a public beheading.

"C'mon, honey. Heard the poor louse on the chopping block is a hydra so it should take about four or five hours to void him out him completely. Seats aren't bullshit, neither. Good view. Best arterial spray for the price."

I declined, as politely as possible.

Thankfully, most of the intense looks during our journey were directed at Palls. A few demons seemed to recognize him and welcomed him the way you would a cop on a beat—a few with silent nods and others by backing up against the walls to escape his path. From time to time, Palls would tip his hat as he walked by as a sign he was just making his way through. Nothing to see here.

"So far, so good," Cain whispered.

Then, suddenly, it wasn't.

A large thud behind us signaled the landing of a Screech. Its black flesh glistening in the city lights, it opened its beak and began to speak.

"JUST FOUND OUT THERE'S A HUMAN WOMAN IN THE CITY. SAD! PEOPLE SAY SHE'S GOING TO DESTROY THE ECONOMY AND I AGREE. FIND THIS LOWLIFE AND TEAR HER THROAT OUT. HASHTAG HUMAN-FLESH-TASTES-LIKE-APPLESAUCE. HASHTAG PAINT-THE-TOWN-RED-WITH-HER-ORGANS."

And then, just like the one before, the Screech keeled over and died right where it stood. A few howls went up in the city as every citizen of New Necro received the same message.

"We need to run," Palls said, dashing out in front before the mob could get moving. "The way down to the Second Circle is right back here."

We ran around a brown-brick building I thought housed a yoga class but was really currently facilitating a corpse-packing seminar instead. When we arrived at our destination, I was too busy running for my life to pay attention to something as trivial as my footing. Luckily, Cain grabbed me and pulled me back in time. "Might want to watch your step there, gorgeous."

She was more than right. I had almost tumbled down into the black, endless nothing of the Maw.

A blast of heat shot up from the chasm like an eternal belch and Palls held his hat in place until it died down.

"All right, Cain. You're up."

"Looks like we'll need to improvise this next part." Spreading her black wings, the angel flew out to the center of the Maw and hovered. "I can't exactly carry both of you for too long, but as long as you don't struggle, we can make it. I'll float us down to a back exit of the Second Circle. Cross will sense us as soon as we step foot in the hotel, but going this route, he won't be able to do anything about it. We can take the next elevator on that floor down to Circle Four."

Cain threw out her arms by way of invitation.

"Yeah, no," Palls shouted. "I'll take the stairs."

"No stairs, big guy." Cain opened her arms again, this time with a taunting smile.

Grumbling, Palls held onto his hat, set his feet, and jumped into the waiting arms of the ex-angel. She struggled with him for a few seconds, and I thought there was a chance of them crashing and burning. But, showing some of her superhuman strength, Cain steadied herself and held out her other arm for me.

Taking one look into the Maw, I called to her. "I'm pretty sure I should've gone first."

"I'll catch you, Grey. Just hop over."

"Sure. *Hop*." Bracing myself, I ran a few steps and jumped—right at the exact same moment a black cloud of Screeches flew up from the Maw. Falling short, Cain caught hold of me with one hand, but the violent winds of a hundreds Screech wings flung us into a midair tumble. It felt like we were in the eye of a wild shrieking hurricane.

Somewhere in that chaos, something grabbed my foot.

Grasping my ankle was a pale blue man, naked and blathering. I had absolutely no idea where he'd come from. The only thing I could guess was the bastard had leapt off of one of the Screeches on the way up.

"If we keep going like this, we'll both fall, you idiot," the man clinging onto me had the (blue) balls to shout.

"Good point," I replied and swung my free heel right into the side of his head, caving his skull in as easily as if I had kicked a wet paper bag. He kept clawing at me, mushed head and all. Eventually, he bound himself around my other leg and, holding onto the entire lower half of my body, the weight was too much to bear. I screamed as I slipped from the angel's grip, plummeting like a stone into the Maw surrounded in nothing but black. Black. Black.

All I could do was stare up as the city lights became smaller and smaller.

Now the size of my hand.

Now just a pinprick.

Now gone.

EPISODE FIVE:
HELL HATH NO FURIES

It's hard to tell how long I was falling. With no light, no sound, and no sense of direction, it almost felt like I was weightless and free. Yes, freedom. Even though I was plunging into a never-ending abyss, there was an odd joy to the way my arms and legs swept against the air—the way I twisted this way and that, leaving everything to gravity.

Falling without purpose or direction reminded me a lot of what it felt like to carry anxiety around all the time. It usually felt like some invisible, impossible beast was chasing me. Other times, it felt like I was plummeting towards my doom, weightless, and waiting to crash.

The other thing about being surrounded by pure darkness: you can't tell if your eyes are closed or not. You kind of just stumble about, half drunk, half dreaming.

And the worst wakeup call you can receive from this existential stupor is standing up and stubbing your toe on the edge of a piece of furniture. It's the kind of thing where your mouth is filled up with hexes for every salesman, every Ikea, every motherfucker who had ever called themself a carpenter for building whatever the hell you hurt yourself on.

That's what happened to me. I don't remember hitting the ground, just kind of "waking up" from landing. It was so dark I couldn't see my hands, even when I felt my finger touch my nose. So when I say I got up and instantly toppled over a hard something-or-other that then proceeded to tumble down with me, it truly wasn't my fault. Feeling it with my hands (and face) told me the culprit was a wooden chair. Not my lamest enemy.

The sound of my voice sounded muffled in this dark space. I couldn't tell if it was my throat or my ears not working properly. In my mind, if I had actually survived the massive fall into the Maw, it meant I had landed somewhere in the hotel and that Mason had already captured me. As I searched around in the darkness for an exit, I envisioned him ordering his patrons to sharpen their knives for another bloody meal. I felt like, sooner or later, the shadows were going to claim me every bit as much as my anxiety had always wanted to.

And I was not fucking going to let that happen.

A blur of light spawned in the air in front of me. It was an image of two girls sitting at a table—one older, one younger—both writing in their notebooks. Flat and partly translucent, the image was familiar and yet so fleeting. As if it was projected into the air itself, the light slipped quietly between the spaces in my fingers.

But then a force took over. As if latching onto my outstretched hand, I found myself being sucked into the image itself. The next thing I knew, I was standing right in the middle of the small living room space with the two girls.

I recognized the room. This was my parent's apartment. This was where I grew up. Remembering it had been destroyed, I realized this was not an alternate dimension or a trick of the mind. More importantly, I realized who these girls were—and had no idea how I'd missed it before.

The smaller of the two was Petty. There was my little sister, maybe at age four or five, strutting around the house in pigtails and the jean jumper Mom loved to throw on her when she was insistent about getting dirty. Petty was the epitome of a town boy and never met a houseplant or crayon she didn't want to decorate the apartment with.

Whatever this memory was, younger Petty couldn't see or sense me. It was almost as if I were walking inside a playback I had been edited into. I was a ghost in my own memory.

The girl in the side seat was, of course, me. Observing how I was slumped over a book with my hair forming an iron wall around my face, it didn't take me long to remember this moment. It was not a good one.

In the memory playback, Petty tapped my shoulder. "Come play," she pleaded.

"Not yet," younger me replied stiffly, lifting one hand to my temple. I remember not wanting to move my head too much.

Petty let out a long wail and my mother ducked out of the kitchen. "Mandy, go play with your sister."

I was stunned to see my mom. In truth, it hurt—even it was just an image of her. Part of it was because it been so long since I'd seen her, but it was also that she looked so young. She wore jeans (when did she ever wear jeans?), a fitted blouse, and her hair was blonde with only the earliest traces of grey peeking out around her forehead. I don't remember my mom ever being so young.

"Doing homework," younger me replied curtly.

"You've been on that all afternoon." Mom walked toward the table. Watching myself, I never realized how uncomfortable I came across. I thought I'd played it so cool, but how could she not know something was wrong? But she did. She reached out and pulled away the hair that was blocking the hideous swell over my right eye.

She sat in the chair beside me. "Another fight?"

I shook my head, but that only revealed the black and blue swelling over my left eye.

Mom reached out, pushed aside the book, and clasped both of my hands in hers. "Tell me the truth, Mandy. Were you fighting again?"

"I wouldn't call it a fight, per shhhhay," I answered, now unable to hide my missing tooth.

Naturally, Mom freaked, but not in the way I'd thought she would. Not even twenty-four hours later I had found myself sitting across from my principal. I didn't say a word. My mom and dad said it all. That marked the last day of school I ever attended.

From that day on, I was homeschooled.

The image vanished and I found myself spit back into the darkness like a big fat loogie. I may have not had a heartbeat built into this faux body of mine, but I laid there feeling as if the edges of my existence were throbbing in the darkness. Every inch of me hurt and radiated with pure pain.

Over the course of what must have been hours, this cycle repeated over and over again. A long time would pass in the darkness, then a hazy fog would show me an awful memory, I would get sucked into it, only for it to spit me back out after it was done and leave me alone again.

I lost count around the seventeenth trip down Mutilated Memory Lane. Soon I found myself talking to myself—to no one. These memories featured all of the Amanda Grey hits: grade school screw-ups, playground fights, that one time Pretty forced me to double date with her and I ended up setting the guy on fire.

This last is in no way sexual, by the way. The schmuck got too close and I chucked a dinner candle at him, end of story. Sure, I didn't know his dense cologne—an aroma which smelled a lot like steroid-induced testosterone and non-consent—mixed with his billowing and exquisitely groomed chest hair would make him go up like a douchebag-o-lantern.

Still, watching "Grey: This is the Crappy Existence You Called Your Life" segments was exhausting.

Even though the pain kept swelling up, over and over, I shouted into the darkness, "Hey, Cross. Are you doing requests? It's just this is supposed to be Hell, *the* Hell, and I was kind of expecting … I don't know, something better? Now, I don't want to tell you how to do your job, but if this is how you torture folks down here—with a glorified slideshow presentation of a person's fuck-ups—then I don't think you've done your homework. Screwing up is kinda my thing. Superman flies. Batman punches people. Amanda Grey burns down half the East Coast casually refilling an ice tray."

Still nothing.

Another memory came, this time of my thirteenth birthday when I threw up all over my mom's homemade cake.

"Good talk," I mumbled to the darkness.

The memories steadily climbed up my timeline until they finally reached something that was disturbingly recent and fresh: the night I met Gaffrey Palls. By then, I must have seen more than a hundred of my memories, and yet this one felt more raw than any of them.

I saw myself staring into a mirror trying to practice smiling.

Then I heard the three knocks that would change my life forever.

I saw myself walking to the door, opening it, and letting Palls into my small apartment. Letting him into my life. I watched the fight that had happened next. The broken wrist, the shattered glass. Somehow, watching it from the outside made me even more uncomfortable. Palls beat me within an inch of my life and yet out of pure dumb luck, I had somehow survived. I should have died that night.

Everything played out the way I remembered. Palls falling to the ground holding his throat. Me crawling to the side with my own breathing problems.

And then there were crows. Five (and then six, of course).

Barnem brandishing a bat.

The money.

The decision that would change—and ultimately end—my life.

This memory marked the darkest part of my life, namely, the last. I don't want to say watching these were anywhere near torture, but they were definitely unpleasant. Every time Barnem showed up, I wanted to spit at him. Every time I saw my parents, a lump grew in my throat thinking about my dad dying.

And there were the other folks who played a role in my life, making brief appearances over what would end up being the last few days of my life. My Super, Lou. Burley's. For some reason, Burley's was a weird thing to remember because I never really got to know Pops and his wife, Lady, just their tasty BYO-ingredient burgers.

Finally, Donaldson. Seeing him again was tough, especially considering the last time I saw him, he had been smashed into a wall. He was always so nice to me, and generally for no reason. It drove me freaking crazy. In my experience, people weren't just nice for no reason—but Donaldson had been.

"You were a good guy," I said to his face as the Amanda in the memory tossed him a specially made burger. I closed this sentiment with, "You big doofus" because it still felt like the right thing to say.

The fall of each Shade.

Petty dying and then undying.

D's transformations.

Each memory played out in the same horrible fashion.

Everything led to the standoff in Saint Patrick's Cathedral. The warrior angels. Barnem cutting off my arm. Bill and Ada, the freakish looking angels that turned out to be the new owners of Heaven (whatever the hell that means, no pun intended). I had only managed to beat Barnem by sneaking those demons inside of me, a little trick D had helped me pull just before we got there. I mean, I had died so I'm not one hundred percent sure I could call that a victory. But I also knew Barnem had lost, and in the end that was all that had mattered.

As the image of D holding my lifeless body faded away and I was vomited back out into the darkness, I felt the silence of the world crawl back around me. I laid my head down, thinking it was better to sleep than to continue staring at nothing. But sometime later something else appeared.

Something I didn't recognize at all.

As I was pulled into this memory, I looked around, confused by my surroundings. I was standing amidst rows of newborn babies resting in a hospital nursery. Some were fussing, others dozing.

I shouted to no one, "Hey, whoever's handling the projector up there, you botched this one. This isn't one of my memories."

The lights weren't completely off in the nursery, and the few that were on cut shadows across the room. For some reason, my vision lingered on one specific corner, gravitating to an empty space where the edge of a table met the wall.

What was there? I stepped closer to get a better look.

As I did, the lights snapped on and a nurse appeared. The sudden sight of her scared the crap out of me and I cleared my throat as if trying to save face, though I was technically a ghost in this memory. She didn't notice me, and I hissed at her to move because she was blocking my view.

The shadow I had been keeping an eye on didn't disappear when the lights came on. Instead, it just kind of squirmed like a centipede thrashing against the floor. Like me, the nurse hadn't noticed it either as she backed out of the room and killed the lights.

I watched as the black silhouette peeled itself away from the wall and grew in size, lengthening from an insect to a fat black, shadowy snake. It slid across the floor, toward a cart with a sleeping baby inside.

"Oh shit. Wait. No!"

I knew it was only an image I was seeing—that I was not really there—but I lost myself in the moment. I jumped up and started waving my arms like I was trying to get someone's attention. But nobody came. I tried kicking and punching this creature, but I slipped right through its body.

I screamed and screamed.

Even as the shadow crawled up the bassinet leg.

Even as it poured itself onto the small child's body.

No one came to help. No one saw. No one knew.

The lights flickered and then everything went silent.

The memory spit me out and I collapsed on the ground, understanding what I had just seen. The baby in the bassinet was me.

I CURLED UP into a ball and stayed there for ... I don't know how long. The memory projections didn't go away, either. After each brief darkness, they flickered on and dragged my prone body in for another round. The cycle restarted at least five times with the residual pain afterward doubling and then tripling each time I was spit out.

When I wasn't trying to shield myself from having to endure the memories, I couldn't help but stare intensely at them. Eventually, I figured out the truth of what I was being shown. Yes, they were displaying every botch I'd ever made on my timeline, but this unpleasant trip down Memory Lane was also revealing what was behind my less-than-stellar moments.

A Shade.

Every time I saw myself, I could spot a flicker of darkness radiating from me, just on the edges of my body. When I was younger, it was a dark outline over my skin and clothes, but as I got older, the aura had grown larger. Vaguely, I remembered being told by a cultist this aura was how dark things found me—angels and demons alike. I was just never able to see it until through this shadowy lens.

The only time I'd ever felt the dark powers inside of me was when it was at its strongest and most volatile—when I had intentionally taken the five Shades inside myself to face Barnem. Now, in this memory, I could see the darkness leaping out of me. What was once a faint outline became a raging black fire that surrounded my entire body. Thinking back, I could remember feeling the intensity of this power threatening to tear me apart. I also remembered feeling it corrupting me, slowly eating away at me from the inside. At the time there were only thoughts and far-off whispers, but I felt them reaching out, hungry fingers and mouths. Something inside of me called me to burn the world down.

And, just when I was done remembering that lovely little stain on my life, the reel started over and it was back to the nursery.

I couldn't watch this part. Not anymore.

I must have cycled through the entire timeline at least a hundred times before I grew numb. My extremities felt as heavy as stone and ached horribly, but I couldn't feel anything inside of me. Something changed and I blocked everything else out. Whatever Mason was doing to me was supposed to douse every ounce of will I had left. But for some reason, something welled up from my insides that reminded me of the darkness I felt in Saint Patrick's. A power? A fire?

Whatever this reserve of energy was, it only made me more focused on what I needed to know. Watching baby Grey inherit a Shade of the apocalypse no longer hurt. It just made me want answers. Where did this Shade come from? What were the Shades, really? I wanted answers—and there was only one guy who could give me what I needed.

But first, I needed to get out of here.

Around the two-hundredth cycle or so, something changed. A sound was coming from the darkness. It sounded like breathing—very deep breathing—from somewhere behind my head. The sound would only happen when one of the memories was playing, so at first I thought it was coming from inside the images. Then, when I tried to pinpoint the breathing, I found it didn't actually sound like a breath at all, but like someone hissing at me, saying, "Hey."

I managed to pick my head up and to hear the breath more clearly.

"Grey?"

I stood up. "Who's there?"

I heard a struggle on the voice's end, like it was trying to pass a stone the size of a bowling ball. Then, out of the blackness, a hand surrounded in pure fire appeared out of thin air. It pulled and pushed the

darkness aside, and then, sliding slowly against the shadow, Gaffrey Palls entered the black space and landed—terribly I must add—flat on his face. Straightening himself out, he tossed me a thumbs-up.

"I'm in."

I crossed my arms. "Congrats. Now get me out."

Palls took one look at me and then another look around the room. Shaking his head, he started swatting at the air like a cat.

"Uh, Palls?"

"Yeah." Pawing, pawing, pawing.

"Did you hit your head too hard? Should I be worried?"

"Shut up for a second." Palls continued swiping at the air, spinning in place as if he needed to touch it all. But when his hand struck something, I realized he'd been looking for an object in the blank space. Sighing, he stood up straight and flicked at it with a fat, sausage finger.

The sudden shock of sight nearly bowled me over. We were standing in the center of a rather plush apartment of all white: furniture, walls, ceiling, artwork, vases. It was easily one of the poshest spaces I had ever seen, and the complete opposite of the dark world I had just been trapped in.

Palls dropped his hand from the light switch. "Let me get you a drink."

"Wait, stop! No freaking fair! Where did this come from?"

Walking over to a stainless steel fridge, Palls pulled open the door and plucked a beer from the shelf. He tossed it over and grabbed one for himself, cracked it open, and then, after chugging a few deep swallows, wiped his mouth with his sleeve and asked, "Tell me you found the light switch?"

I pointed behind me. "I didn't … I wasn't …" I stuttered before settling settled with "I found a chair" as if this was better than nothing.

Not amused, Palls pulled a chair from the glass table and took a seat.

I considered my beer. "If these aren't our real bodies, and we don't eat or drink, can we get drunk?"

"Nope. Other beings can, but not us." Palls took another swig from his bottle. "Doesn't even taste like anything, really. But it's one helluva thing to savor."

I popped my lid and downed the entire thing in one gulp. He was right. Being stuck in a corporeal body meant I might have had sensations of liquid going down my throat and maybe a strain of taste behind it, but it was nowhere near the kind of alcoholic experience I was hoping for. What Palls was actually savoring was the action of drinking—the normalcy of the practice. It was amazing. Just feeling the liquid against my lips, flushing through my teeth, was met with a glorious feeling of the familiar.

I realized this was what people referred to as "longing for the departed."

I also realized I was the "departed."

Finished savoring, Palls pushed aside his empty can with two fingers and then interlocked them. "We need to get you out of here."

"Obviously, Palls. Mason has been trying to mess with my brain this entire time, so I'm looking for some payback."

But Palls only sighed. "This isn't the Third Circle, Grey. Turns out you fell all the way down to a city on the outskirts of the Fourth Circle. We are in Mischief—the Under Dweller City—and it's … not the best of places. Right now, you're being held as a prisoner, but I'm not sure why. Haven't been able to find any word on the Warden of the Fourth, either."

"Your Warden babysitter buddy? Can she get us out of here?" I gulped down the last of my beer. After crushing the can with one hand, I shot it at a nearby trashcan and missed by about ten feet. I left it there.

Palls looked at the crumpled can on the floor and back at me. "If I can find her. But before we break out of here, we got something we need to talk about first."

I stretched. "Yeah, well. I have quite a bit to talk to you about, too. This can't wait until we're out of here." I paused long enough to see that, by his body language alone, whatever Palls had to tell me was eating away at him something fierce. I sighed. "All right. Out with it, then."

Palls pointed at the can on the floor as if this was his most pressing concern, but I just kept staring at him. When he saw I still wasn't budging, Palls got up and threw the can in the trash himself. In a partial grumble, he told me, "I guess there's no way around this now, so I might as well and come right out and tell you. You're a Warden of Hell, Grey, just like me."

Gaffrey Palls might as well have punched me in the face.

For what it's worth, I took it very well.

"You're fucking kidding me! I swear to God, you'd better be fucking kidding, Palls or we're about to have a major problem."

But Palls only blinked at me.

I got up and started pacing. "I-I can't be a Warden of Hell, Palls. I'm from Queens."

The tall man shook his head. "I don't see how that—"

"You didn't think of sharing this tiny detail with me *sooner*? Like, a lot fucking sooner? How the hell did this happen?"

Taking his seat again, Palls explained, "Like I told you. Shades infest the soul, corrupt it, and paint it black. Not only do folks possessed by Shades get a one-way ticket to hell, but you also get a job to do when you get down here."

"Fan-freaking-tastic." I closed my eyes and let out a long, deep sign. "Do you have any idea which Circle I'm in charge of?"

"Not sure. Somewhere down where I've never been. Now, I'll be honest. I don't know much about what goes on below this city in the Fourth Circle. I just know things will start making less and less sense once we get closer to the bottom. Look, I'm only telling you this because it's bound to come up sooner or later. Our priority is to keep this under wraps for as long as we can. That means until we find the missing Warden and skip out of town as quiet as we came in. First order of business is getting you out of here."

"And how do we—?"

Before I could spit the rest of my question out, we were interrupted by another round of memories. Another dose of "Screw-Up Roulette" was about to start, but this time there were two images: one for each of us.

Palls looked caught off-guard. I watched him snap his fingers and manifest two floating tongues of black flame, but before he could use them, one of the memories began to suck me in. I saw a large, smoking field and heard the rattle of gunfire, but this wasn't my memory. It was Palls'.

Palls reached out to grab me, but it was too late. Another image popped up behind him—a memory that was mine—and the two forces pulled us apart and into each other's own respective, personal Hells. As soon as he vanished into my memory, I tumbled into his.

I landed in a burning field where there were trees torn from the ground and smoke rising from the scars of artillery fire. A tank battalion rattled in the background and invisible planes boomed overhead. In front of me, a soldier limped into view and then fell face-first into the war-scorched earth.

When I came to Hell, I had expected a fight for my soul.

I didn't expect to watch the last will and testament of Gaffrey Palls.

I STOOD OBSERVING as Palls rolled onto his back and stared up at the sky. The clouds were gray and lifeless as if painted into place. With his body wrecked, his left arm filled with shrapnel, and his entire uniform soaked with blood (some, he assumed, his own and some from others), Palls felt he could've stayed planted in that dirt for years, but it's crazy how quick you'll get to your feet when the sound of unfriendly tank treads roll nearby.

Private Palls held his arm in place and forced himself to his feet. He was bleeding from the forehead and ears, but it's not like this meant much. His entire squad had been blown to bits around him as they helped usher a convoy across the countryside. Everything had been quiet during the ride, a mission that was supposed to be as exciting as watching paint dry.

Then the bombings started.

Bent metal. Burning bodies.

Now the enemy was coming back in with cleanup crews and Palls knew if he didn't want to end up on the business end of a tank shell, he was going to need to move—and move fast. He tried to do so but quickly found breathing impossible. Stripping himself of his field gear, Palls found he could wring blood and sweat from his fatigues, which was in no way a good sign. He must have caught more shrapnel than he first thought. Sure enough, reaching up, he felt a warm, wet spot right below his ribs.

His fingers came out coated with red and he collapsed to his knees.

There wasn't any way he was coming out of this. Not alive, at least.

Nearby, the enemy infantry's shouts could be heard. They were close.

Palls smiled. As a kid growing up in the Bronx, he was familiar with the numbers game. Bullies always rolled in packs in his neighborhood, and this had given Palls an understanding of how things worked. They may have had the numbers, but with the right plan, one Average Joe could be as strong as any army.

"Got nothing to lose," Palls muttered to himself as he drew his field knife. His carbine was gone, but with a little guts and some dumb luck, Gaffrey Palls was going to make sure the dance ticket he was about to punch included a few more bodies.

Palls wriggled to position himself behind a fallen tree outcrop next to a hard bend in the road. He planned to catch the search squad from behind, the nature of the up-close-and-personal fight, taking the tank right out of the equation.

Lying in the mud made Pall's wounds worse. Blood was pooling around his shoulders and exhaustion was overtaking him. He felt as if he could have put all his gear down and sleep for 100 years—more, probably, because he'd very likely never wake up again.

He forced himself not to give in to the lull of sleep, and as soon as the tank rolled by, Palls pulled himself into a squat. When the truck flanking the tank was clear, Palls sprung out and let his knife greet the soldiers bringing up the rear on foot.

In two movements, he drove the point once through an enemy's neck and—while he was still gurgling to death—turned it backward in a swift slice across the fallen soldier's neighbor's eyes, blinding him.

This wasn't the first time Palls had killed an opposing soldier. Nor was it the first time he'd witnessed a man gasp his last breath and fold over. Not by a long shot. It's just the others had been at a distance, bodies dropping out of existence and sent to God through the sights of his rifle. This was the first time he'd taken a life up close—the first time that last breath came with bloody mist he could taste in the air.

To Palls' surprise—and he guessed to the surprise of the enemy—they weren't expecting one man to charge headfirst into them like he did. In fact, from the looks of it, they weren't a search party at all. Not battle-hardened infantry soldiers, the small platoon had been escorting a supply truck.

Before the second man's body dropped, Palls hopped aboard the truck, adrenaline keeping his movements sharp and deadly. There were four soldiers left and while they weren't caught completely off-guard, they hadn't heard the first kill over the tank treads. Their half a second of reaction time was enough for Palls to kill one more soldier before any of the others ever made their move.

Palls had each of the remaining three men by an entire foot of height and maybe fifty pounds of muscle, but that damn numbers game kept its advantage. A shot rang out, but it either missed or his blood was boiling so hot he didn't feel the bullet sink into his body. One carefully executed head-butt flattened a third soldier, but barely before the other two tackled him.

The fight raged on as one storage box after the next tumbled with them over the side of the truck. Palls landed on his neck—damn near broke it, too. One soldier's entire head was pinned under one of the crates and it made a *clop* sound as his body went limp beneath it. The second crate burst open right at the feet of Pall's final enemy, and three sharp knives spilled out blade side up onto the caked ground.

Palls' body was falling apart, his side ready to split open, so he couldn't get to the weapons in time—but his enemy did.

Grabbing one of the blades, a short-hilt dagger, the soldier kicked Palls' body onto his back. Flipping the blade in his hand, the soldier's lip curled into a smile. Then he drove the knife right through Pall's chest.

Gaffrey Palls died on the spot—

—at least that's how everything should have gone down. Instead, as soon as his heart stopped beating, Palls opened his eyes.

On a tree branch somewhere above his head, Palls spotted a large bird, perched on a branch. The world around him was mute as he watched the creature spread its wings and descend in slow motion. Landing on the hilt of his dagger, the large crow stared down at Palls.

With the beak an inch from his mouth, Palls could see that, aside from a white stripe of feathers on its head, the bird had red eyes, each with a number 5 sitting at the center.

Fleshy. Weak.

The voice crawled around inside Palls' head.

Another dying meatbag. Shame, really. Real shame. This cute little war you're having has been entertaining. The Romans knew warfare, though. Up close and personal. Guts and intestines dangling from swords. So much blood soaking in the fields there would be lakes.

Behind the bird's head, Palls spotted the enemy soldier that had killed him. There was something wrong with him. His skin was gray and his body was posed as if stuck in time. In the distance, frozen as they attempted to climb out of the truck as well, were two more frozen, gray soldiers Palls had no accounted for.

Well. It has been great, the crow hummed. *I should take momento. Great wars don't come around too often, and the last guy I was in was blown to bits.* The crow stared down at him. *What do you say Gaffrey Palls? Want to keep living? Of course. Of course. There's too much to be done. There's* so *much.*

The bird plunged its black beak into the wound made by the dagger. The gash ruptured and blood shot from it like a crimson geyser. Palls felt his ribcage crack open as the massive bird slipped its entire body into the gushing scar and vanished into his chest cavity.

Suddenly, sound flooded back to Palls' ears as the world sped back into motion. Leaping up to his feet, Palls felt both pain and power coursing through his body.

The enemy soldier, likely shocked that the man he had just killed was now standing upright with a dagger sticking out of his chest, screamed. Palls' body moved instinctively. With one punch, he sent the enemy flying, the impact launching him several yards away—and not in one piece, either.

The driver of the truck and its passenger, both fully armed, opened fire. Palls closed the gap with ease and shoulder-checked both of them with the velocity of a freight train. One man's body was sent through the truck door and splattered against the inside of the windshield. The other's hit the top of the truck and rag-dolled through the trees.

Palls heard the turret of the nearby Panzer tank turn his way and set its sights on him. Instead of backing up, Palls stood his ground as the main cannon opened fire.

With one hand, he cradled the explosive shell it fired, tucking it under one arm like he was catching a "beaut" from an all-star quarterback. The force made Palls slide back a few feet, but he dug his heels in the ground to stop his momentum and, in one simple motion, leapt a full ten yards onto the tank. Kicking open the hatch and diving in, Palls handed the live round to one of the infantry inside just as the whole thing exploded and engulfed everyone, including himself, in a column of pure flame.

A few minutes later, Gaffrey Palls stepped slowly out of the inferno. His clothes had been burnt to a crisp, but the rest of him wasn't marred by even a scratch. He stared down at his right hand and curled each finger. Reality felt different. Life felt different. Palls felt he could reach out to the entire world, and with his bare hands, throttle it to death.

Palls pulled the blade from his chest and tossed it away. Even though he had slaughtered a small battalion of men, all he could think about was getting back home. He could go now. He could see her.

"Wait for me, Mel," Gaffrey Palls said aloud and then continued, repeating, "There's too much to be done. So much," as the wound in his chest slowly sealed itself shut and the soft hum of a crow echoed in his ears.

As THE MEMORY came to an end, a force spit me back out into the white apartment from before. After surviving one of my memories, Palls landed somewhere behind me. As I tried to get my head to stop spinning, the last thing I wanted to do was stick around for another slide into Gaffrey Palls' psyche.

Like my own memories, I had not only been *in* the projection, but I'd been connected to the living, breathing Gaffrey Palls. I felt his pain. His anger. When the Shade tore into his body, it was as if it was tearing into mine. I had no control. I even felt the rush of power and the sick joy that came with killing those men. I wasn't ready for the thrill of taking a human life, the bloodlust setting all of my nerves on fire.

We both sat there not knowing what to say to each other.

Finally, I broke the silence. "Palls—"

"We need to get out of here," he interrupted, standing and walking over to a wall.

I picked myself up, too. "Yeah, that's what I was about to say."

I understood why he didn't want to go anywhere near the experiences we had shared or what I had to say about his memory. And yet, I had so many questions. The Shade had appeared to him as a crow, but mine was merely a shadow. Why was there a difference? And the name "Mel." Whoever she was, she was important to Gaffrey Palls—or at least she had been. Neither of us was prepared to talk about it though, so we focused on the task at hand instead.

Palls snapped his fingers three times, summoning three flames for each snap. He then spread the flames from his hand up his right arm. When he was done with this neat little magic trick—the same technique he'd used to free us from Mason's trap—his entire arm was set ablaze in a bold column of fire from his fingernails to his elbow.

But, unlike the time before, when Palls sliced the walls, nothing particularly remarkable happened. Sparks flew. Burn marks appeared on the walls' surface. But he might as well have been throwing soggy matches at it. Flustered, he extinguished his arm.

"Your friend Cain was supposed to help us out from the outside. I can manage enough hellfire to get me in, but making a hole big enough for the two of us to get out takes more power than I got. Where the hell is that dumb angel?"

Clearing my throat and standing up straight, I tapped him on the shoulder.

"Wild idea, here."

"The answer is no," Palls responded immediately, but I could tell his back was against the wall.

"You said it yourself, right? I'm a Warden. A Shade Wraith." I smiled broadly. "Teach me how to be a fiery hell spawn." And then I ended it with, "Pleeeeeaaassse."

Palls' eyes went from his arm to me. "Amanda Grey, controlling hellfire?" He stood silently, mulling the whole thing over. Then he passed a hand over his face and groaned. "I'm going to end up regretting this, ain't I?"

I smiled. "Probably, but two Wardens are better than one. It's a numbers game."

I must have been on my hundredth snap. Not a flame. Not a flicker. The most I was able to muster were two strings of smoke rising from my index finger. A hell-born savant, I was not.

During this time, Palls was summoned to his memories on three more occasions. As long as I was far away from the projection, I was free from getting sucked into it. I entered mine and he entered his with no questions asked. Palls always stepped into the memory without resisting, but always came out…different. The first time, he'd picked himself up right away. The second and third times were far worse, and he stayed on the ground for a long time before coming over to help me figure out the flame trick. I never asked him what he was seeing and made a mental note to make his life at least two to three percent less difficult than normal.

Palls trekked over for another beer (which seemed to be in infinite supply) and hunched over the counter.

"How's that going?"

I held up my middle finger and Palls squinted at it disapprovingly. "No flames on it."

"Oh. Right." I flipped to my smoky index finger on my other hand. "I've only been practicing with this one."

Whether he cared for my joke or not, I couldn't tell by Palls' chiseled chin and cheeks. "You gotta understand the way these afterlife bodies work. It sort of feels like you're on autopilot, right? Like you're numb? Use that. Consider yourself a candle no one has lit yet. Not much to you, you're just this useless thing with no purpose yet."

I nodded. "Useless. Got that part down."

He tapped my finger with his. "Hellfire is what lights the candle, drawing it of yourself like a match hitting a wick. Except, of course, that hellfire can burn another soul down to nothing, so just be careful with it."

"You know, you're kind of like my Yoda," I told him. "The only difference is you suck."

Palls sighed. "I don't get that reference, but I'm sure it was witty and somewhat topical. Just focus, Grey. Remember, snapping doesn't create the fire. It's just there to remind you what heat feels like. The moment you feel that friction, feed it. Pour yourself into it. Expand it like a balloon. You said you did this once?"

I looked at him lazily. "Back when I fought the angels and Barnem, sure. But that was by using the other Shades as batteries. I'm just little-old-me now."

For the first time, Palls audibly gasped. "Wait. You're telling me you had more than one Shade inside of you at one time?"

Not understanding why he was freaking out, I nodded. "Except for D and one other who was hiding in a pen... uh, long story."

"So, including yours, you held five?"

"Sure." I shrugged and looked over. "Only one less than you. What's the point?"

I could tell Palls was choosing his words carefully. "I saw... I saw a hospital in your memory."

His words set me on edge. "I don't want to talk about that."

Palls held up his hands. "I get it. I'm sure you saw what I had to deal with. I know it isn't something you want to talk about right now. But I just want to know, how come your Shade didn't corrupt you right away? You had it for your entire life."

I thought for a bit. "There was a phrase Cain taught me back in the land of the living. She called it the 'Subjugation of Wills'. Heard of it?"

"Can't say I have."

"It means that my charming and all-around-shining personality was able to beat back the Shade inside of me. The demon that was feeding off my pain and misery got more than it bargained for and developed its own anxieties. Guess it screwed with the wrong person." I smiled. "Even a Shade can't out gloom and doom me."

I could tell Palls wanted to say something about this, but he changed the subject. "Keep practicing. They should be coming for us soon."

Rolling my eyes, I went back to it. "Do tell, Palls. Who are 'they'?"

"I wasn't able to find the Warden. She's someone I've met in passing. Not a bad gal. I don't know much about what goes down here in Misfit, or in the Fourth Circle, but if the Warden is missing, then we need to be careful of who's in charge right now. This prison is slowly draining us, Grey. We're bleeding out negative emotions and whatever this is—whoever 'they' are—is getting us nice and primed for someone or some*thing*. They don't know they have two Wardens locked up down here. For now, we can use it to our advantage."

Palls walked over and placed a hand against the wall. He pushed and tiny cracks formed in the surface. "This place is built for lost souls, not for folks like us. You must feel the hellfire welling up inside of you, right? It keeps us separate from the rest. Not much in Hell can stand up to us when we are powered. Probably only one group of creatures down here, but we don't have to worry about them."

Palls lumping "us" together was somewhat infuriating, but I kept it to myself.

"My power feels like there's a cork in the supply in here. I'm guessing it's either this room or because the farther away I get from my Circle of Hell, the weaker I get. Either way, that means your power is muffled in here, too. Which is a good sign. As soon as you get out, using hellfire should be easier for you." I tossed him a doubtful look and he added, "Just think of it as training. Like running with weights on."

"This," I replied, snapping my fingers over and over, "isn't running with weights on, Palls. It's more like running without legs. What am I going to fight with my fiery jazz hands of doom?"

"Relax, we got enough time. It's not like they're going to burst in right now and—"

"Prisoners! It's time," a voice shouted.

I rolled my eyes. Of course. If I had a nickel for every time...

A small crevice opened in the wall and dragged itself down to the floor. Four figures stepped through. Two were brown rats riding armored locusts the size of horses. Their ten-foot tails were raised over their heads and their sharp stingers sat pointed at us. Strolling in behind these creatures were two black-clad guards baring chains to bind us.

One of these guards had a very familiar face.

Cain spat and hid a wink behind her scowl. "You're coming with me, prisoner scum."

Our armored escort led us out of the room and through a tear of reality as we stepped into the true version of Misfit, the city on the edge of the Fourth Circle of Hell.

Misfit was nothing like New Necropolis. Where New Necro sported dazzling skyscrapers and valleys of running streets, Misfit was more of a dirt-laced factory. As my eyes adjusted to the dim lighting, I saw hissing steam jets shooting columns of white smoke while silent fans chugged away in the distance. Metal walkways ran in uniformed rows leading upward and downward and sideways across the expanse of grim factory floor. There was an assembly line for objects suspended from metal hooks. Each of these objects was about twenty feet in diameter, black, and circular, but the material wasn't glass or metal. It looked—and unfortunately *smelled*—organic.

I became very aware of the moans and screams coming from the black orbs around us, and, from this, how many of them were housed here. From what I could see—ceiling to floor and wall to wall—there were hundreds of the little black prisons, maybe thousands. They went on forever, disappearing into the distance among the various catwalks. Gazing at their unfathomable numbers, something told me that my previous guess of a thousand was probably missing several zeroes.

"What are these things?" I asked, poking the flesh casing of one of the black balls with my finger. It wriggled, murmured like a dying calf, and went still.

Palls looked around. "This is what they kept you in. They house small folds of reality. Infinite space in a finite package. They call them Black Bladders."

I sighed. "Not sure who's in charge of your PR department down here, Palls, but I would make some phone calls. Or write a letter to someone. Calling these things 'Black Bladders' has got to be the worst combination of words I've ever heard. That's right up there with 'Phlegm Slurpee' and 'Thong Song.'"

"Shut up!" Cain yelled at us. She was on edge. The rats on their armored steeds made a tight lap around us, while the guy walking beside Cain— a lobster-man in a black turtleneck—didn't seem to care about anything.

I couldn't see where the danger was, but around us the temperature spiked as three very loud *put-put-puts* cut the silence and a fiery tear sliced open in the walkway above. The flames crackled and flickered as three figures emerged onto the metal grate a few steps ahead of us.

Cain waved and her lobster coworker pushed us behind a wall and out of sight. Making sure we ducked our heads, it also gave our chains a meaningful tug to make sure we kept quiet. The locusts bore their stingers at these three new guests. From my vantage point, I could see little more than their outfits. They each wore heavy black coats with high collars that blocked off their faces. Two were tall and slender; the one standing in the center was as broad as a small couch. Their voices were female, but not entirely human.

"We shouldn't be here, sister," one confided to the next. This voice sounded filled with gravel, but her coat moved as if there was something struggling to get out. I thought I heard the muffled giggling of children.

"She finds us here, sister, and she will be angry," spoke the second in a much more melodic voice. Purple hair sprung out of her high collar. Defying gravity, it was roughly the length of my entire body and it swayed, weightless, as if viewing coral underwater.

The shortest one took a few steps forward and stepped up to Cain.

"We would like a word," she said. Unlike the others, this one looked and sounded human. She sported dead white hair and her collar was partially down, exposing nothing of her face but her milk-white eyes.

"You are not allowed here," Cain ordered, her voice shaking terribly.

There was a quiet standoff and the fear was palpable. If something was scary enough to frighten Cain, the former Angel of Death, then I knew it must have been bad news.

As if she hadn't heard Cain at all, the sing-songy sister with the wavy hair informed the others, "Let's go, sister. We will have our time with her. Besides, I'd rather not be around these Bladders. They smell of human skin and pickling regret." She backed away from one and her hair moved with her as if in agreement.

"We should go, sister, before the little ones get hungry." From under the taller one's coat, I heard the chattering of teeth.

Even hidden behind one of the steel walls, I could feel the sister's eyes piercing into me. I could see them in my mind. They were glowing and did not blink. These creatures were here for me and everything about them screamed violence and torment.

Seconds ticked by without a word from anyone. Then, I heard the *put-put-put* sound again and the portal swallowed the dark trio up.

I couldn't believe how much these three women, if that's what they were, terrified me. Even with the massive amount of oddball shit I'd seen in my lifetime, the thought of being in the same room with those three again nearly brought me to tears. If this is what Palls claimed life was like without a Shade to warp and distort my emotions—if this is what True Fear felt like—then my journey to the heart of Hell was going to be harder than I thought.

It didn't help when I looked over to Palls, his eyes showed nothing but fear.

"Who were they, Palls?"

"Those where the Furies," was all he said.

The rest of the escort went off with more surprise visits, but thankfully none from the murderous trio. Toward the back of the factory, the Bladders ran for what seemed like miles. Scattered amongst them were misshapen creatures that seemed to be human—if humans could have been wadded up into sacks of their own skin. These creatures had no hair, no eyes or body parts, just round heads with skeletal mouths and full, pink stomachs. Jutting out of their oval bellies were sharp hook points suspending them from the ceiling, like Christmas ornaments at Hannibal Lecter's house.

Passing underneath these horrors dangling at eye level sounds pretty terrifying, but the truth was that the only one that seemed disturbed by any of this was me. They just hung there, muttering to themselves about gas prices, people not curbing dogs, and the price of cereal.

"It's a *six*-dollar box with a *two*-dollar taste," one of them chattered to no one in particular.

On her way through, Cain accidentally bumped one of the meat pods and sent it rocking off to the side, to which it snarled, "This may be a site of unspeakable torture, honey, but manners are free. The only thing you gotta pay is attention."

After making our way through this grotesque menagerie, we passed an area without any Bladders. The entire space was hollowed out with hundreds of armored locusts on patrol. On guard as well were the massive rats. Just like the one that had been sitting at the preacher's feet in New Necro, they all wore tattered clothes. Their fur was matted and smelled rancid, and they stared at me with beady red eyes as I marched by.

At one point, I even heard one tell the other, "That one is a female."

"Ugh," its neighbor responded, shielding its eyes with its pink hand. "Looks dirty. I honestly can't look at them for too long. Gives me the creeps."

"Excuse me," I shouted. "I can hear you, you know?"

Both rats jumped to attention. One said, "It's yelling at us. I think that's a sign it's ovulating."

"I think I'm going to be sick," the second one yelped and skittered away looking for a barf bag.

The rats themselves seemed to be tending to a large collection of objects growing from the floor and ceiling. At the center of this den was a large stockpile of putrid looking eggs big enough to encase a human

being. There were covered in mucus and rotting flesh encircled the base of each egg in a death hug. I could see, even in the low lighting, shadows curled inside their fleshy interiors jerking this way and that.

When we stopped for Cain to speak to another guard, I backed up to where Palls could hear me. Just as I was about to ask, a few of the eggs ruptured, emptying their content of yellow slop and passengers onto the ground with a rotten barfing noise. Some rats came over and quickly began scratching and pawing the residual tissue from these creatures. I couldn't see what these beings were exactly, but what I did see was enough to turn my stomach—not an easy thing to achieve, by the way. Standing to their feet, the three newborn figures spotted us and approached.

"What are those things, Palls?"

Gaffrey Palls spat. "The worst of the worst, Grey. Give me demons any day before having to deal with these things. And it looks like they're making an entire army of them down here." And then, as our new guests stopped a foot from us, he spat again: "Trolls."

As they came into full view, I saw that these "trolls" were some of the most ordinary-looking people I'd seen in what felt like ages. Unfortunately, that wasn't saying too much.

The man on the left wore a hemp shirt and I could see yellow teeth on the other side of some wickedly chapped lips. He caught me staring and grabbed at his crotch. "Hey, honey. I'm down to fuck. You down to fuck?"

I nearly lost it. "*What* did you just say?" My voice came out in a shriek.

But this only brought the attention of his neighbor, a skinny guy with a comb-over and dead shark eyes. "I wouldn't hit that," he howled. "She looks like a bitch—and she's fat."

My mouth hanging open, I spun on this one and was ready to punch him, when the third—a tubby round kid, roughly sixteen to seventeen years old—added for no reason, "I personally think Episode I and II are the superior *Star Wars.*"

"Oh, that's strike three, motherf—"

But Palls grabbed me by the shoulder before I could ground that freak into the dirt.

"Don't feed the trolls, Grey."

Our trek continued as Cain led us up a thin walkway through the back of the troll-hatching chamber. I couldn't help but wonder how she had landed a job in the Fourth Circle. Walking behind her, it occurred to me that her resume must have the most impressive things on any plane of existence. She had a plan, and it was almost impossible to get her to talk, but she'd left clues.

Back amongst the Bladder, as she snapped our rusted shackles together to bind our forearms to our lower backs, she had told us, "Look at your face. Been down here so long you can't even speak." And as we walked, she kept making comments like, "These guys' brains are mush. Look at them. They can't even fight back."

Both of these were obvious words of warning.

Don't act up. Lay low.

Palls must have understood this, too. I knew already it would only take a blink for him to slice everyone in half, but he kept his mouth shut and did as he was told.

Cain walked ahead. Her coworker—the lobster looking monstrosity with beautiful blond hair and broad shoulders—brought up the rear. I took the opportunity, with my hands pinned behind me and obstructed, to practice the light trick. But no sooner had I formed my fingers to snap, Palls rammed me with his shoulder. He played it off like he had stumbled, but I could tell by his face he wanted me to stay away from practicing anything with people nearby.

Our destination came up at the very back of Misfit. Running in hundreds of designated rows, a long system of pipes ran forward a few yards before dropping into the ground. The pipes were rusted over and seemed ancient, but one sported a hatch with an opening large enough for someone to climb into.

So, naturally, the first thing Cain did was swing open the nearest hatch and cackle. Even when she removed our chains, she kept on cackling.

I swear she was enjoying this act *way* too much.

The lobster creature reached for something but Cain declared, "I'll bind these two," and whipped out two silver collars lined with black runes. Her lobster coworker waived his head, swung his antenna around, and gurgled, but Cain rolled her eyes. "Really? I think you should leave it to the folks with hands, pal."

Dejected, the lobster person looked down at its claws and emitted a faint sob.

"Behold, you idiots," Cain exclaimed holding the collars for us to see. "The Binds of the Fourth Circle. These will keep you stupid and docile. The moment you do so much as flirt with common sense, your mind will be bombarded once more by the images you have faced within your Black Bladders. They will remind you how pathetic your life really is."

Chuckling to herself like a villain not even a community theater would find credible, she looped the collar around my neck. Just as she made to fasten it, her fingers jerked in one extra movement. I caught it. She hadn't clamped the collar down, so the whole contraption just kind of hung around my neck without actually being locked in place. She did the same to Palls' piece and then threw her hands up to exclaim, "Now go, sheep! Cower in the face of my Lord. The Scourge of the Sectarian. The Embodiment of the Immoderate. The Signer of my Paychecks."

She cackled again and tossed her blonde hair around like a shampoo commercial for sociopaths.

"Hey, Cain?" I whispered. "I think you're operating at about an eleven."

She winked as if this were a good thing.

"No, you idiot. Don't wink! That rating is out of three!"

Cain's eyes shifted between the pipe and me, a clear sign that I should shut up and climb in. Nearby, her lobster pal curled its eyes at me. Palls and I did our best zombie stumbles into the pipe and laid flat. Just before Cain shut the hatches down on top of us, she glanced down, flashed me a thumbs up, and then with both hands shut Palls and me into total darkness.

Cain's voice lingered outside, muffled but distinct, until it slowly died off and vanished. From his own pipe, Palls called out to me.

"Hey, Grey."

"Yup."

"I kind of hate your friend."

I didn't want to agree with him so I kept my mouth shut.

"Let's just be ready for any—"

I never heard the rest of what he said, because the next thing I knew my body was shot through the pipe like a bullet.

THE PIPE SPIKED left and then right. At one point, it spiraled upward and then it dropped down bobsled style.

After a few interesting winding turns, I dropped right into a cushioned seat. Palls landed in a seat beside me and we realized that—much to our mutual horror—we had been spit out in the middle of a studio audience. Our neighbors around us were all human and, from what I could tell, just as confused as we were. There must have been over a hundred of us, fired out of the overhead pipes like spuds from a potato gun, and dropped into stadium seating chairs. I noticed everyone was wearing Binds of the Fourth Circle, only theirs were fastened correctly. Outside of these seats was a vast sea of blackness in every direction. It was as if we were floating in space.

"What is the meaning of this?" one man screamed. "I was a respected man of the clergy. I gave my life to the Church."

"I shouldn't be treated like this," a woman chimed in. "I was a doctor who dedicated her life to cancer research and medical aid for underserved populations."

"Hi, my name is Chad," a third man explained with a wave. Everyone stared at Chad. "I, um, don't belong here either, or as well, because I just never really left my house. Not sure why I'm being tortured if I mainly stayed in my mom's basement and drank soda. You know, living my best life."

Everyone waited for him to sit down and shut up.

The crowd started to argue, everyone trying to voice their concerns about their afterlife placements, but before it got out of hand, the little runes and scripts on the collars flashed gold. At this, everyone sat down and shut their mouths—even Chad. Palls and I made sure to sit as still as possible and do our best to blend in.

Rushing toward us was a red wall about twenty feet tall. It was as if it were flying toward us from miles away, but at Mach 5. It stopped just short of the front row and I recognized it as a curtain, one that parted as soon as a giddy little piano showtune began to play.

Behind the curtain was a stage featuring a u-shaped desk and curved chair that made it look like any run-of-the-mill evening talk show. Suspended over the chair, through thick black cables that snaked high into the air, was a helmet-like contraption. Behind this stood a backdrop featuring the silhouette of a sparkling cityscape, and above, a sign was lowered that not only let us know what we should do next, but was reinforced by a foursome of rats riding giant locusts who appeared on the sides of the stage and demanded:

"APPLAUSE!"

They snapped their tails at us threateningly.

"APPLAUSE!"

The collars clicked off and everyone, dazed and depressed, began to clap. One man broke down crying and the locust closest to him impaled him through the face and flung his body to the side. Almost instantly, a new nobody was spat out into the vacant seat and, unsurprisingly, she started clapping right away.

A fiery tear *put-put-put*'d itself on stage and out stepped a woman—half of one anyway. She wore a black dress that wrapped around her body in thick coils. Her right side was smooth and flawless, and jet-black hair spilled down to her waist. A beautiful ice blue eye sat next to a sharp nose, while her left side was … I guess the word would be "nonexistent." Mostly it was just loosely knit gray nerve endings and withered bone. Side-by-side, this creature was half-gorgeous while her other half looked like a plate of worms passing around an eyeball like a beach ball at a concert.

She reveled in our applause. "You're too kind. Too kind." Holding up her rotting arm, she bowed to our forced reception. "Honestly, too kind. All of you."

We clapped harder.

"No, seriously! Cut this out! It's too kind!"

She pointed at a man who was clapping too graciously and a large hound the size of a horse leapt from out of nowhere, mauled him to death, and dragged the corpse back to the stage before beginning to play with it like a pet-store chew toy. We all clapped a little less enthusiastically as a replacement audience member was plopped into his recently vacated place.

Our hostess returned to being jovial. "My name is Hel, and thank you for joining me on 'The Hel Report.' We have a great show for you tonight, so let's jump right in."

I couldn't help but notice how half of her face was smiling and the other half was busy trying to hold her teeth in place. She tapped the hound as it played with the severed torso and performed a silly dance back to her desk. Nine television screens appeared hovering over the stage and each one showed close-ups of various angles of Hel's face.

The hound in the corner was truly monstrous. The matted brown fur running along its body stopped around its massive black paws. With six red eyes—three on each side of its large head—it watched us all carefully.

Hel clapped gleefully. "First, I'd like to thank you for checking out my channel. 'The Hel Report' is the number one watched streaming torture channel in all the Circles, and I couldn't have done it without all of you." She blew a kiss and some of her lips fell off. "And, just to show my love for my die-hard fans, my ride or dies, my 'Hel-Heads' out there, I'm giving out something special to the first ten people who press the red button on their armrests. That's right, smash that button. Get a gift."

The entire audience looked around. Ten buzzers sounded as ten buttons were pressed, causing a series of blades to drop down from thin latches in the ceiling and behead the button pressers as they sat in their seats. Someone beside me had been one of the lucky (or *un*lucky ones, not sure) and his severed head bounced down the steps like a giant meatball covered in loose hair. I could see the dog on the stage twitch with desire.

"I feel good about tonight," Hel told us with a smile.

Rats appeared from the side of the curtain, carrying the bodies of the dead to the front where they piled them like discarded luggage.

"Tonight, I'd like to talk about something near-and-dear to my black heart—and something everyone is talking about nowadays: the state of Hell."

Everyone in the audience looked at each other. Were we talking about that?

She looked at the audience. "I'll tell you what, and excuse me for getting a little 'real' with you right now." As if to better catch the power of her emotions, the images of the television screen flashed through several filters until it landed on a somber sepia. "I remember the heyday of Hell. Back when everything was just torture and strife and disembowelment, you know, when things were *simple*. Back when names meant something—like the Valley of Infinite Screams or the Cave of Endless Wonder." Hel paused on this last. "On second thought, a den where you're rectally fed snakes until your stomach bursts should have had a better name slapped on it. I'll admit our PR department needed some work."

I elbowed Palls to show him that someone else agreed but he just hissed at me.

"My point is this: what happened to us? Only the Old Ones—like me, like my brother Fen here—know how glorious damnation used to be."

She pointed over to the hound quietly gnawing on a skull and then sighed, causing a puff of moths to flutter out of her dead cheek in the process.

"I'll tell you when it all started. When the world of humans almost ended on earth. Then all of a sudden, we were saddled with Wardens. Shade Wraiths. Who voted for *them* to be in charge? Why did *they* get jurisdiction over the Circles of Hell?"

Using her dead, bony finger, she tickled the top of the desk. Instantly, it grayed and withered. Hel stood up just as the wood collapsed in a rotten heap. "Before them, the Seven Dragons held dominion over the Circles of Hell, and they haven't been seen in ages. And now look at me.

Me! In charge of the Fourth Circle: The Abaddon of Have's and Have Nots. Pathetic! *I* should be in charge. *I* was here before all of them. I mean, you can't even spell 'Hell' without 'Hel'."

The APPLAUSE sign lit up and we all did as we were told.

Hel acted as if she were genuinely taken aback by our praise. "I know, right? You get it. You get it. Who better to lead you than me? Lucifer? Ha! He thinks he can vanish for a few thousand years and then send Screeches out expecting the hordes of Hell to bend to his will? Torture isn't a hashtag. And that's why, to commemorate the success of 'The Hel Report,' I am announcing an expansion of sorts. I'm going *viral*."

Grabbing the cabled cap from the air, Hel placed it on her head. It seemed like the entire world shuddered as purple energy currents arched out from the cables. It dawned on me that this was why the Black Bladders were syphoning energy from us. That was their purpose.

Whatever energy was pumping into Hel was also rising out of her mouth in a green cloud. Drifting onto the pile of corpses nearby, the green mist quickly settled into their expired flesh. And then, one by one, the bodies stood. From out of their bloodless stumps, where their heads had once been, sprouted large cameras draped in colorless flesh. The cameras swiveled back and forth for a while before setting their lenses on their master.

"What would I be without Followers?" Hel cackled.

"We gotta get the fuck out of here," I whispered to Palls, who nodded in immediate agreement. As soon as we stood to make a break for it, a familiar woman appeared, carrying a spear in one hand and a card in the other. Cain dashed passed the hound, which snapped at her heels, and handed Hel the card only to turn and disappear behind the curtain again.

Hel read the card, passed it to her dead hand, and watched it disintegrate.

"What the hell is your friend doing," Palls whispered to me.

I was too scared to respond. I didn't have a clue anyway.

"Funny." Hel walked over to her brother, the hound called Fen. Giving the audience her back, she whispered something to the beast that made him stand and bare his teeth.

"Funny, funny," Hel repeated as the hound prowled to one side of the stage.

To my left, Palls' fingers were a blur. He snapped his fingers five times and wove the tiny tongues of flame into a single ball of black fire in less time than it took to suck in a breath. He kept it low, between his knees, biding his time for someone to make a move. I thought about snapping my fingers, but I knew my little light show wouldn't compare to his and I didn't want to make us look bad.

The veins and nerves throughout Hel's body began wriggling as she climbed the steps on my right. The hound was mirroring her up the left. Behind them both, trolls and rats and even Hel's Followers were spreading out in case anyone tried to run.

"I guess it's fitting," she said, still speaking to the audience. "Here I am talking about the no-talent Wardens, the useless Shade Wraiths of the underworld, and we're in luck. That's right. We have *guests* in the audience tonight."

The two were only a row from our seats when Palls stood up. He tossed the fireball at the hound's head and pulled me to my feet.

"Anyone you prefer?" he asked.

I slipped by him, yelling, "Fido."

Palls ran toward Hel and I watched as the hound huffed up its chest and blew out Palls' black fireball in midair like a child playing with a dandelion.

With Palls and Hel mixing it up, all six of Fen's red eyes locked on to me.

I stopped short and started running back toward Palls. "No fair! Switch back! Switch back!"

Hel reached into her mouth with both her living and dead hands and pulled out two swords—one gold, one bronze. She brought both blades down on Palls who blocked both of them with an arm encased in fire.

Through his gritted teeth, he yelled, "Kinda busy here."

I turned back and Fen the hellhound was sizing me up. The audience was already running for their lives, but the hound either swatted them aside with its paw or ignored them. I was its prey—lucky me.

"I killed the Warden of this floor," Hel shouted as she put more pressure on her dual swords. "That's right. I hung her limbs to decorate my foyer. And I can't wait to add two more prizes to my collection."

Struggling, Palls fell to a knee. His fire began sparking as if about to go out.

Hel was ecstatic. "Wardens or not, you can't kill an Old God."

"Palls!" I was caught between a hound and a hard place. I didn't know what to do.

And then Gaffrey Palls said three magical little words:

"Light them up!"

As I turned back, Fen had already leapt high into the air.

I raised my hand and snapped my fingers just as the beast was close enough that I could feel its hot breath on me.

I only got one shot off.

The largest ball of fire I'd seen Palls produce was roughly the size of a basketball.

The only way I can describe what leapt from my fingers was that it was definitely round, but only in the way a gaseous planet the size of a small woodland cottage is.

Even with the beast's enormous size, Fen hit the ball of fire and was immediately engulfed by its flames. It let out one pitiful yelp and vanished. The hound's flaming corpse didn't even come out of the other side. Instead, the sphere continued on its trajectory, broke into the edge of the stage, and exploded, raining black jets of flame down on everyone's heads.

Hearing two swords clatter to the ground behind me, I spun around to see Hel and Palls gawking at the destruction I had caused.

Shaking, the Old God dropped to her knees and screamed her brother's name. She began raking at her face and hair, cursing in a language I was pretty sure hadn't been spoken in eons, and Palls picked himself up as we both dove through the massive hole my little light show had produced.

Making it outside, I was immediately stung by cold. The building we had escaped from was nothing but a square void planted into the dirt—a windowless, thoughtless black cube. But the real oddity was where this place was located.

Outside, a moon and a vast night sky hung above our heads. For a moment we just stood there, staring up at the twinkling stars and the moonlight. In the distance, we saw mountains and endless desert rolling in every direction. I couldn't tell if I was still in Hell or not. The rest of the humans made their way out behind us.

A peal of tires broke everyone's malaise. Folks scattered. As Palls and I watched, a beat up, dusty green car with awful wood paneling right out of the 70s squealed to a stop in front of us.

Cain popped the passenger door open.

"That was easy," she grinned. "Get in."

We drove for a long time without speaking: Palls in the backseat laid out, me in the passenger side staring out the window. Only Cain, still wearing her black uniform from another failed job placement, looked even remotely pleased with herself.

I didn't know what was on everyone else's minds, but in my head I kept replaying the image of my hand nuking a giant dog. Part of me wanted to test snapping my fingers again, but I was afraid of the whole "blasting a hole in reality" thing.

The road seemed to run on for ages. I wasn't sure about the gas situation, but I thought this was the least of our problems. The shitty car kept thumping and stuttering as if it were going to fall apart at any minute. Still, Cain kept her foot on the gas and never dropped below ninety.

We drove until the night spun over. I watched as the sunrise changed the blue sands to a blazing orange color I'd never seen before. The cold of the night seemed like an afterthought after driving for minutes in the strangling morning heat.

The desert was vast in every direction. I rolled down the windows to get some air, but the sand flying in felt like glass shards on my skin. There were no plants or animals, no signs of life in any way. In the distance, five steep mountain ranges could be seen, but other than that brief bit of punctuation there was nothing else to be seen for ages.

After a long while, I decided to break the ice.

"Hey, Cain."

"What's up, love?"

"Just for my peace of mind. What was your plan back there?"

"You mean my rescue plan?"

I nodded slowly. "Sure."

Cain seemed extra pleased with herself as she leaned into me. "I planned to infiltrate their ranks. You know, get on Hel's good side?"

"Wait," I cut in, a sudden thought forming in my mind. "How is it that you get all of these jobs down here?"

"Two words: Fallen. Angel," she said, pointing back at her wings. "Hell loves its Fallen Angels. I didn't even have to interview for the last gig. But anyway, after sneaking into the establishment, I planned to get you reunited with Palls, make sure you were in the audience in front of Hel, and then boom!" She slammed both of her hands on the steering wheel and then offered me one of her palms. "I will accept praise in the form of high fives."

I tapped my forehead instead. "Where does the 'boom' come in, Cain? Can we unpack the 'boom' for a second?"

"Old Gods are ancient beings of pure evil," Palls told her as he sat up. "Generals of the Dark Lord himself. Plagues of humanity. We could have been torn to pieces."

The ex-angel clucked her tongue and peeked at him through the rear view. "And here you are bitching about it, Palls. C'mon! Both of you kicked her ass and got out of there. Bet Hel and her demon dog will think twice about coming up against two Wardens next time."

Palls and I didn't respond.

After a minute of the open road and the thumping from the car, I asked, "Do you even know where we're headed, Cain? Is it that way, toward those mountains?"

"Those aren't mountains, Grey. And we're headed to the Fifth Circle: the River Styx."

I looked around at the rolling dunes and blowing sands.

"Where's this river?"

"No idea," she said, and then seemed to remember something. She slammed on the brakes, skidded to a stop on the side of the road, and hopped out. That's when I realized that the banging sound wasn't coming from the car.

It was coming from its trunk.

So, a naked blue man, an ex-angel of death, a guy with the powers of a demon inside of him, and I were riding in a car…

There was a joke in there somewhere, but I didn't exactly feel like sticking around for the punch line.

The blue man sat in the front with me. While he had absolutely no problem with his nakedness, I made sure to keep my knee from rubbing against his. Bony and wispy, his skin was as thin as paper, so much so that the wind blowing in from the windows and hitting his flesh made it sound like the dude was a kite caught in a high-powered fan.

"Where did you get yourself a liar?" Palls asked.

"Don't look at me," Cain deflected. "That's the one we crashed into back at the Maw."

Peeking over at him, I had to ask, "So, you're really a liar?"

The blue man shrugged. "Yes."

I narrowed my eyes, not sure if that was a lie or not. "What's your name?"

He thought about it for five long seconds and then responded with a shrug and a name that clearly ended in a question mark. "Mark?"

"Thanks. I regret asking." I grabbed "Mark" by the shoulders and forced him into the backseat. "Now, can someone please tell me what this guy has to do with where we're going?"

Palls pushed the little guy to the other side of the backseat. "Liars have their own place in Hell, Grey. They're tortured in the Eighth Circle, which means—"

"Which means if he was able to come up, he can show us the way back down," Cain finished, way too happy with herself. "Now speak up, little man. Are we headed the right way?"

Not-Mark leaned forward, squinted, and sat back with his arms crossed. "Yes?"

I raised my hand as if in class. "Okay, can I point out something that may or may not be a horrible problem—one I feel we may be overlooking and which might lead to our eventual doom? This guy—the guy we're basing this entire ride on—is a *liar*."

"Whoa," Not-Mark shouted. "Ouch."

I was beside myself, having left any last bit of my limited supply of patience back in Hel's bizarre studio. "I didn't make that up. That's literally what you call yourself!"

"Just drop it for now, Grey."

I turned back in my seat to shout at Palls, but stopped as we locked eyes. His stare told me everything I needed to know: he was far less concerned about the paper man beside him as he was about me annihilating a supposed eternal deity of the underworld with a simple, totally unpracticed gesture. I sat back down and faced forward. "How far until we get to this river?"

Not-Mark decided this was a good time to be cryptic. "Distance isn't real. This car isn't real. This desert isn't real. What you're looking for will appear or it won't appear. It might take minutes or never. We drive until the end."

It's difficult for me to explain, but somehow, the liar was telling the truth. We rode on and on and on. The days changed, from night to day and back again. But the five shadowy mountains in the distance never moved. Neither did the road or the car or sand. It was all just empty flatland in front of us for ages.

After what felt like days in the car without anyone saying a single word to anyone else, I turned to riddle Cain with another bevy of questions, but I stopped short when I saw the lifelessness in her eyes. The angel's face was pale and she seemed to be dozing at the wheel.

"Hey Cain, you feeling okay?

Startling her caused her to spread her wings. One smacked me right across the face and the other shattered the driver-side window. Cain slammed the wheel so hard to the right I thought we were about to flip and tumble. But she turned back, swerved to get back into position, and continued the course.

"My bad," she protested, but immediately started to fall asleep again.

I grabbed the wheel as she slouched over into my lap.

That's when I saw it. Around her collarbone was the wound I had spotted back in her apartment, only now it was the size of a fist. Even worse, around it the skin was cracked and gray. Whatever the wound was seemed to be spreading under her armpit and behind her neck, crawling over her body like an infection.

The car veered again and started to fishtail wildly as we hopped off the road and into the sand. We were completely out of control now as Palls and I tried our best to wrestle the wheel into the right position.

"Her foot's on the gas pedal!" Palls yelled as he dove into the front seat. With all of Cain's weight on me and my mouth full of her feathers, all I could do was stare out at the land in front of us.

Something caught my eye. Even in the brightness of the daylight, I could see an object streak across the blueness like a comet. At first, I thought the yellow beam was a star rising high into space, but it became painfully obvious as it got larger and larger—swelling from the size of a penny, to that of a bowling ball, to a house with white boards and large windows—that whatever it was coming *toward* us.

The star-turned-building landed with a large, earth-shattering crash in the dirt about fifty yards ahead of us and we were still speeding toward it going a hundred miles per hour.

"Balls!" I shouted.

Palls shouted back. "Almost got it!"

"I didn't call you but yeah, hurry the f—"

"Done!"

Palls struck the brake, sending us into a sudden wild skid. With the small house coming up on us fast, I held on for dear life—or, whatever—as the car sent us into so many spins that I lost count.

Finally, the car came to a stop and everyone let out a collective groan.

All except Cain, who popped up immediately.

"Cool. We're here," she said and climbed through the broken window like this was no big deal at all. As she walked away, I pushed open my door and tumbled out onto the sand with much less tact.

After a minute or two, my legs and arms were working so I decided to use them. With my hands firmly affixed on my waist, I followed the skid marks we had made in the sand. It was quite a long walk, but as soon as I stepped back onto the black tar road we had been driving on, I glanced both ways and screamed my frustrations at the open air. It was the same in both directions: a dark, dead vein running across a brown, cracked land.

I had expected to get through the Circles of Hell one-by-one, busting down one door after another and taking on any and all types of weird that came my way. What I wasn't expecting was entire worlds to trek across, Old Gods, and miles and miles of nothingness.

My hands started to shake so badly that even the sky itself seemed to be throbbing. This wasn't like any panic attack I ever remembered having when I was alive. I just kept pacing and breathing until Palls approached.

"How are you feeling Grey?'

"Me?" I replied. "Look at me, Palls. I'm fucking fantastic! Just leave me alone for a bit."

Palls didn't budge.

Still pacing, I asked him, "What was Hel trying to do back there?"

Palls shook his head. "She was building a legion of trolls and what she called Followers—an entire army for herself. Looks like she's planning to invade the other Circles of Hell."

I threw my hands up. "And that's totally normal? You're completely fine with that?"

The older man crossed his arms. "I'm not, but I've also been down here longer than you, which means I'm used to things literally going to hell on a minute-by-minute basis. If you really need to know, it's worse than I thought, okay? Hel was able to kill the Warden of this Circle. That's not something that should happen. The Old Gods created Hell; they travel in and around it. They stir up trouble from time to time, but nothing like this—and I've never heard of one killing a Warden. So, yeah, something's *really* wrong down here, but I also know it's not going to get any easier." Seeing the pain on my face, his voice took on a softer tone, "Roll with the emotions, Grey. It'll pass. Don't fight it."

"I'm sorry," I wheezed. "Tell me again when was the last time you blew up an Old God?"

"Um. Never. Actually, that's not supposed to be possible."

"Great."

I tried to walk away, but Palls maneuvered in front of me. "Just take it easy. I'm just asking for you to listen."

I wanted to lash out at him again, to remind him to keep to himself, but instead I took a deep breath. It felt like my brain was on fire, like my insides were drying out. Even if I wasn't in a real body, I constantly felt like I was being shoved through a meat grinder.

"I know you're not looking for any advice, especially from me, so take this however you want. Leaving all of that mess inside of you isn't going to make you saner. You need to get those emotional knots out of your system."

Palls crossed his arms and straightened his back, just like I had seen him do a hundred times before. I understood what I needed to do. Slapping my hands on my knees, I bent over and stared into the black road. The two of us must have looked like two of the most amazing idiots in Hell: Palls the dumb statue and me in my doped-up ostrich pose, but I truly gave no shits about it.

In a rush of hot air and even hotter fluid, whatever anxiety had been pooling up in my joints was suddenly flushed out. It felt freaking wonderful.

"Does that help at all?" Palls asked.

"It will if you shut up for five seconds," I replied. After those beautiful moments ticked out, I stood back up and let my hands slide up my thighs and back to my waist. The world was calmer; my nerves were not firing off like fireworks. I didn't feel like the entire world was trying to swallow me up. For the moment, I seemed to be back to my new normal. "Okay. Let's get back in the car."

Palls sighed. "Not possible. Mark and your feathery friend went inside that diner."

"What diner?"

The "diner" was what had landed in front of our car. The place was a

large, oddly-angled establishment made of white painted wood and sporting broad windows that displayed the shape of patrons—most of which had wings—sitting at booths. A big fat black sign pointing down at the diner's roof dubbed this place "Slice of Heaven" with a wedge of orange pie beneath it.

As I gawked at its sign, Palls pulled up beside me.

"I know we got a lot to talk about, and hell, I don't even know where to start. But let's slap a rain check on that. Right now, we're still in the Fourth Circle—still in Hel's reach—so we're not out of the woods yet." If that wasn't ominous enough, Palls stared at the diner. "I've heard rumors about this place. The only establishment in all of the Nine Circles that's run by angels, the Fallen kind. I don't think I have to tell you they're not going to be too kind to the two of us. Just stay sharp and maybe … I don't know, act normal." With that, Palls grumbled under his breath that he could use a beer and made off toward the diner's front door, leaving me completely alone on the strip of road.

I bent back over into my "What-the-Hell Ostrich" position and muttered, "Fucking angels."

A ROUND WOMAN sat on a round black stool by the front door of the diner. Without saying anything, she counted us four, snagged a corresponding number of menus, and led us to our booth. As soon as we slid into our seats, I took a good look around.

The diner looked like every other diner I'd ever been to: a single row of stools for solo eaters, small tables for pairs, bigger booths for larger parties. On the walls hung pictures, not of people, but of pies: pumpkin, chess, pecan, and key lime, to name a few. At the far end, fastened to a wall, was a television. Definitely not of the flat screen variety, this massive hunk-of-junk was playing a single show.

"*Full House*?" I exclaimed, keeping my voice down. "A diner run by angels in Hell is playing *Full House*?"

I thought my voice was low enough to not be heard beyond our little circle of weirdos, but nevertheless the entire diner went quiet and all the angels stared in my direction. Actually, stare is not the right word. Rather, everyone stopped what they were doing and tilted their heads, wings, and bodies toward me as if waiting for me to say something else.

Cain cleared her throat. "*Full House* is a perfect show, Grey."

"Y-yeah." I nodded. "Totally."

The entire diner went back to what they were doing.

Wanting to take my mind off of that, something from the first time I met Cain stood out in my mind.

"Hey, Cain. Didn't you say angels don't need food?"

Cain smiled broadly and looked ravenously at the menu. "This is a pie and shake place, gorgeous. Pie and shakes ain't food. And guess what, they aren't served in Heaven, believe or not. Order whatever you want. It's on me."

I had a hard time accomplishing this. It wasn't that any of it looked terrible, it was just that the whole menu was written in an odd language. From the pictures, the pie pieces looked enticing.

Our waiter stopped in front of us. He looked human, but his neck was stretched like he had swallowed an umbrella. Surrounding his throat, hovering where his Adam's apple should have been, was a gold ring. The angel flipped his notepad closed while cringing with obvious distaste at our party.

"I'm sorry. Who are ya'll with?" he asked with a heavy seasoning of snark.

"Oh, forgot my halo," Cain exclaimed, removing a gold ring from her left ring finger. As if it wasn't made of metal at all, she pulled it open to fit over her head. Stopping it around her neck, she gave our waiter a mildly salacious wink. Displeased he couldn't just kick us out, he rolled his eyes and asked, "What can I get you?"

"Bah! Three of everything," Cain replied before anyone could get a word out. Then she added, "and throw four drinks for me in there. Make 'em strong!" The waiter scooped up our menus and trotted away.

The place was packed. From the counter to the booths, every seat was taken. There were angels with and without wings. There were malformed angels, ones with long, swollen arms and others with feathery tails. All of them wore their halos around the neck instead of hovering over their heads. Regardless of what they looked like, it was obvious they wanted nothing to do with Palls or me. I could feel their eyes lingering on us from time to time and their gazes weren't particularly friendly.

Needing to ground myself, I asked, "Mind explaining what this place is and why we're here?"

Cain tried to laugh it off. "Beats the cats in Olive Garden, eh?" Neither Palls nor I broke so much as a smile. "You guys are the worst. All right, fine. This place is the reason I followed you all here. We angels call

this the 'SoH.' It serves as a place for Fallen Angels to transition. It's like a sentient pie and shake palace; it moves around the Fourth Circle, helping out any Fallen that shows up." She flicked her ring/halo and it wobbled back and forth around her neck.

"What kind of 'transition' are you talking about?" I asked.

Cain looked at me, eyes half-lidded. "In my case? The one into the unemployment line."

The waiter came by and served up fifteen small plates and four drinks. I wasn't sure how this all fit on the table, and to some extent, it didn't. But we made do. The pies themselves looked edible, but I was too caught up with what Cain reached for first to have a chance to consider tucking in.

With one hand, the ex-angel of death downed an entire drink that suspiciously looked like a concoction of blood, skin, and hair pureed into a small mason jar. I was so horrified by it I think my internal panic button broke. I just sat there on permanent pause, mouth open and eyes fixed open.

Wiping her crimson mustache, Cain belched. For the first time, I became truly aware of Cain's other-worldliness...her strangeness. Even with her wings out all the time and her casual demeanor surrounding everything having to do with the afterlife, it was something I had taken for granted.

The other thing I had been taking for granted, and which became painfully clear watching her slurp down bloody meaty bits, was that while my corporeal body was built with pain and suffering, it wasn't built with a gag reflex.

As she grabbed another one to down, I grabbed her hand to stop her.

"Cain—and I mean this from the bottom of my heart—what-the-fuck?"

She blinked at me. "You don't like the pie?"

"I'm sure Grey's referring to the cup of mutilated meat you just downed," Palls explained, obviously wanting to throw up himself.

The angel sat back against her seat. "Fine. A little Afterlife 101. This is the Fourth Circle, also known as the Abaddon of the Haves and Have Nots. Story goes, Abaddon was the name of the largest angel to fall from Heaven during the Great War. Abaddon was massive, an angel who could

only be measured in centuries. Think about that—a being who wasn't *miles* long, but measured in *lifetimes*. Anyway, he fell and landed here, but instead of rising again, Abaddon sunk into misery for everything he and the reset of the Fallens did and did not do. So, instead of moving the poor lug, the architects of Hell built this entire circle inside his bones and flesh. Those five mountains you saw in the distance were the fingers of his left hand."

"So we're inside a giant, decomposing angel?" I closed my eyes. "I feel like a broken record here, but did you ever think it might be nice to share this kind of information a bit earlier?"

"Didn't come up," Cain replied glibly.

I nodded, but mostly because the mason jars full of human bits was immensely gross. "And what's that got to do with the guts-in-a-cup?"

"The Fourth Circle is where we angels end up when it's all said and done," she explained, "This place is for our transition into the ranks of demons, suffering, and minimum wage. You all may have corporeal bodies, but angels are ethereal. We were made perfect and that cannot be undone, hence the need for these pretty things." She held up one of the bloody cups and I thought I spotted a fingernail swirling inside. "On Earth, I didn't need food to survive. But in order to stay here, angels must defile ourselves. It's either that or we turn to ash. That's why this place is so important to all the angels employed down here. Without it, we would cease to be."

She pulled open her collar to show us the gray hole and her cracked, dying flesh. It began blooming with color, a clear sign that her drink was doing whatever it did to heal her.

"Cheers!"

With that, Palls and I were forced to watch as she wolfed down another entire cup in one big gulp. Between the hearty slurps, I saw the other angels all had crimson filled cups of their own. After a large, satisfied gasp, Cain held up the empty cup in mock salute and added, "And they serve it in these little mason jars. Ain't this adorable, Mark?"

The blue man, who hadn't been paying attention this entire time was caught rubbing his tongue on what looked like a cold slab of lemon meringue. He sat up and nodded agreeably.

"First of all, stop calling him Mark," I snapped. "He's not Mark. He's the un-Markiest person I've ever met. Second, you're right. These mason jars are pretty damn adorable and I wish I had these in my apartment back when I was alive."

"Why do you sound so angry about it?" Palls asked, squinting at me.

"It's how I started this conversation and I forgot to change my tone. Lastly, why is it that I can't have an uneventful afterlife? Didn't I meet the 'fucking weird' quota back when I was alive? And what do you mean 'perfect'? Most angels I see are..." I flipped a look at a particular angel in a corner booth. While her body seemed normal, her face looked as if someone who had never met a human being in their life had put it together. Her eyebrows and eyelashes were switched, her mouth sported no lips to speak of, and her eyes were *literally* drawn on. In fact, they were drawn in with pink and purple ink to look infinitely attentive to whatever was being said.

Cain laughed. "That's a testament to your kind, not mine, darling. The holiest of beings have no grasp on human anatomy so their attempts to blend in, well, totally suck."

I knew firsthand this was the truth. Cain and Barnem looked very-much-human, but they had been hanging out with my kind for a while. Those weirdos who showed up just before I died—the new owners of Heaven— looked like terrible renditions of actual humans. They had reminded me of starved owls stuffed into human flesh, and not very "angelic" at all.

I glanced toward the bat-wing doors that led to the kitchen area. As a waiter pushed her way through, I saw a few people running back and forth. Two faces in particular seemed very familiar. For some reason, I could have sworn I saw the married couple that ran my favorite burger joint back in Queens. It was for a fleeting second, but they sure did look like Pops and Lady slicing pies. As I sat up to take a closer look, the doors stopped swinging and I lost sight of them.

Confused, I sat back down. "Hey, Cain. This place serve anything other than pie and shakes?"

The angel downed her third cup. "Nope."

I sighed. "Can't believe I'm saying this. I mean, I knew I'd miss the whole 'living' thing. I knew I'd miss my parents and, yeah, part of me even misses the shit-show only New York could supply. Never thought I would be fantasizing about Burley's though."

Palls tossed me a side eye. "What's a Burley's?"

I sat, flabbergasted. There was no way Palls would have known about my favorite little eatery, but still.

"Burley's is a burger joint. *The* burger joint. You bring in your own ingredients and Pops and Lady cook it up. Onion rings. Potato chips. Beef jerky."

"An undead bird."

I shrugged. "Whatever floats your boat, Palls."

The man rolled his eyes. "Not what I meant. Heads up."

Palls gestured to a black shadow whizzing by the diner. It took to the air once more before plummeting into a window, sending hundreds of tiny shards of glass everywhere by the far end of the diner.

The Screech landed with a large clatter on the back of an angel, driving his head into his blackberry pie and probably killing him in the process. With its big leathery wings outstretched and its black skin hanging limply off its bones, the bird opened up its large beak and cackled:

"I JUST HAD AN OMELETTE. IT WAS WEIRD AF BUT WHAT ELSE WOULD YOU EXPECT FROM A BREAKFAST MADE IN HELL. HASH TAG ILOVETHESMELLOFSULFERINTHEMORNING

It then died on the spot.

All of the diner patrons went back to their food and conversations.

Seeing the bird flop onto the ground while an overworked angel broomed its carcass aside, I just had to ask, "What's the point of all the Screeching? Isn't he the embodiment of evil? You'd think he'd have better things to do with his time."

An angel with long earlobes—ones that hung so low they curled out onto the table— peeked out at me from the other booth.

"Hey, buddy," I shouted over, "Don't you try to angel-shame me. I'm not siding with the guy. I just think he should get his priorities straight. Go back to your pie."

He looked away and Cain added her two cents. "Might want to keep that under wraps, Grey. We may be Fallen Angels, but we don't side with the Dark Lord."

"Blah. These people hate me anyway. And don't forget that I'm what I am because of the delusional righteousness of an angel. If you ask me, Good and Evil run on the same schedule. Sometimes, it's hard to tell the difference. What's wrong with a little blasphemy?" I asked, looking at everyone in my party.

Cain tapped her fork over to a sign hanging over the head of the short angel who'd seated us. On a finished wooden frame, the phrase "HOME SWEET HOME" was painted in bold blue lettering. And, on the bottom, scratched in with a sharp blade were the words "Except for blasphemers."

"Oh, c'mon. Give me some space on your soapbox. I'm not saying anything everyone isn't already thinking. Hell has always been sold as a place of endless fire and torment. So far, I've seen more torture filling out warranty contracts at electronics stores. If this place is Hell, what is Heaven?"

As soon as that comment landed, as of punctuating the end of my sentence, something struck the side of the diner so hard, everyone's plates and cups were launched into the air and came crashing down onto the floor.

Cain, wide-eyed, immediately looked at me. "Grey?"

I put my hands up. "Wasn't me."

Out of nowhere, the television attached to the wall at the far end of the diner let out a high-pitched wail. The screen burned a white color and then the static of snow.

Onscreen, Hel appeared. The non-decaying side of her face seemed to have been crying and her voice trembled with both rage and pain.

"Hello, Hel-heads. I come before you today to declare the end of my highly popular and frequently watched show. I just can't go on." She bowed her head and started screaming.

"SHE KILLED HIM. SHE KILLED MY FEN. THE ROTTEN BITCH KILLED MY BROTHER."

When she swung her head back up, Hel's eyeball had sunk deep

within the twisting nerves. "At least that's what I felt. But just now, a curious Screetch just arrived, addressed specifically to me. And it came bearing the name of the person I want to eradicate."

A chill ran through my body as Hel positioned herself *really* close to the screen.

"Amanda Grey, I've found you."

Suddenly, the television jerked to the side and split open. A body unfolded from it— female, muscular—but its head remained the broken television set. Just like the camera-headed creatures from Hel's show, this one had been turned into one of her Followers.

An angel stood from his table and conjured a large golden whip out of thin air, but the television-headed Follower proved too fast. It drove its arm through his chest, tearing off one of his wings in the process.

The diner exploded into a panic as, from the windows, several dozen camera-headed Followers, armed rats of Misfit, and trolls poured in. Palls set three of them ablaze as they tried to jump Cain, and scythe in hand, she clove two more in half—though she seemed distracted by the other cups on the table.

"This can't be happening," she screamed, slurping one down before the table imploded under the weight of four trolls. "*Friends* was an overrated show," one troll yelled as he grabbed my hair. I stabbed him in the eye with a fork and scrambled away.

My entire party rushed out of the door and bolted to the car. Not-Mark leapt into the backseat and I flung myself into the passenger side. Only Cain remained behind. She stood by the door, fighting off one wave after another. There must have been over fifty disciples of Hel fighting the other angels inside and, in the distance, I saw a small army shambling its' way toward us.

"Cain!"

The angel wasn't listening, so Palls grabbed her by a wing and threw her into the car. Sliding into the driver's seat, he didn't even wait for us to close our doors before hitting the gas. In a flash, we hit the sandbank and landed back on the road.

Cain looked out of the back and began to sob as Hel's army plowed

into the walls of the diner like a wrecking ball. As we sped away, we could see angels being dragged out onto the desert and killed. Some trolls climbed the Slice of Heaven sign, tipping the whole thing over and sending it crashing through what was left of the roof.

It was at that moment—the moment where Cain lost her only chance to survive in Hell—that I realized every Circle was closing in on us. Even if I did get to Petty, even if I did face down the Dark Lord, how I was going to get us out?

We drove for what felt like days. Palls rolled up his sleeves and took off his tie. Cain, in the back, stayed silent. I wasn't sure what to tell her to make her feel better, so I kept to myself. There was no sign of Hel's army or any other life, and there was no way to make sure we weren't being followed. So, we kept driving.

Muddled within this dread and doubt, with the endless nature of Abaddon and the fallen angels, I had honestly given up hope of escaping the Fourth Circle.

That is, until we reached its end.

In the horizon, the landscape vanished. Palls made a stuttering sound and everyone in the car sat forward as the road dipped out of sight in a smooth decline. We took a hill, and emerging over its crest we saw what was waiting for us.

We were still miles away, but the world in front of us was a gray mass, a sea as far as the eye could see—an entire ocean that had been summoned from out of nowhere.

I spun back to our guide. "I thought we were headed to the *River* Styx.

Not-Mark casually flicked his blue finger to the body of water in front of us. "This is it."

It took us ages to actually get to the beach. The road ended and I couldn't recall there being any space for turns or coming traffic. It was as if the road were set down for us to go to that specific place at that specific time—kind of like Not-Mark had implied earlier.

As our odd-looking crew left the car and started down to the beach, I stayed behind to take a good look at the thankless chariot that had brought us to this place. The fender had fallen off. Rust had eaten away at the doors to the point most were missing their handles. The tires were all flat and weeds had grown up and into the axel. The question I was left with when I walked away to join the others wasn't how this contraption had gotten us here in one piece, it was how this car was able to move at all.

I found my crazy troupe staring out into the ocean. Not speaking, not moving. I wanted to tell them about the car we just left. "Hey, guys. Just saw something that kind of freaked me out."

Then I looked out to the sea and froze.

Up close, I could see the ocean wasn't made of water.

It was made of bodies.

Gray, swollen bodies. Millions and millions of naked, hairless corpses piled atop each other. Men and women, swirling about. Swerving back and forth as if on a current. Rising in waves and crashing down against the shore in ragged lumps before being dragged back out to rise and fall again. If water makes a dashing sound as it splashes about in an ocean, the sound of a million bodies crashing into each other just sounded like someone stirring a wet bowl of spaghetti on a speaker turned up to max volume.

What made things worse was that the corpses weren't exactly dead. I mean, they were all definitely removed from their mortal coils, but they seemed completely content with how bad their situations were. They stared at everything with yellowed eyes but offered no complaints, only a dull grunt or two when they butted heads. Then a quick sorry cleaned it up and nothing else was done.

"What the hell is this?" Palls asked. He looked ill. Even Cain looked disturbed by the sight of this, and she had "heaven-sent reaper" on her resume.

The four of us stood there, on the edge of the Sea of Corpses. We had no way across and no way back. Without saying a word, I already knew. Everyone was too afraid to ask, but I knew.

I can't tell you how much this tore the resolve from my body. I hadn't given up when up against a city of demons. The terribly named Black

Bladders hadn't stopped me. I even killed something that was supposed to be eternal and hardly had time to process it, before this. This was the absolute low I was so afraid of feeling. Getting to Petty in one piece and facing up against the Dark Lord was already a long shot.

But this ... this was worse than anything I could have imagined. To me, this was a reminder of that girl I saw replayed in the Bladders. Amanda Grey: the fire starter. Amanda Grey: the self-imploder. "Mental Mandy" strikes again.

Frustrated that no one was saying anything, frustrated at the sea, and more importantly, frustrated I was unable to finish what I started, I picked up a large, smooth rock from the ground and launched it into the ocean.

It sailed high and carried far. Everyone watched it make the distance and then turn sharply downward before plummeting into the corpses. The result was not the soft thud I had anticipated, but a distant "ow" by one of them. On the heels of this came an eruption beneath the surface of the bodies. It shot hundreds of the flopping corpses into the air as if a bomb had gone off.

At first, I thought it was my rock, but just beside the high arching cascade of corpses rose the nose of a wooden ship. The mass of this vessel coursed through the corpses as if on actual waves, tossing the poor schmucks aside with its keel and punctuated by the odd *plops* and *oofs* from the folks it was rolling over.

The ship looked like someone had bound a scrapheap together and set it afloat. Its wooden planks and railings seemed to be held together with nothing but good intentions. Three massive sails made of black fire slipped open from its masts and began fluttering in the wind.

And then, from out of the main cabin, a lone figure stepped out to greet us. He wore a long black pea coat with the collar up around his ears and a black knitted cap on his head.

"Are you just gonna stand there or can we get going? Parking's kind of a bitch around here," D shouted.

And then he waved at me and gave a simple, "Yo."

And all I could do was wave back. I'd never been so happy to be rescued by a demon.

EPISODE SIX:

WHEN DRAGONS COME BACK TO ROOST

FROM THE DECK of the ship, I watched as land slipped coldly into the distance, grew small, and vanished. This was the last memory I had before setting out from Abaddon to the River Styx—now the Sea of Corpses.

Everything changed once the land disappeared. There was no sun out at sea. There was no moon. The sky itself was endless gray and black cloud cover with strips of purple thrown in, reminding me of dead veins hanging limply from the sky. Any semblance of normalcy I had felt in the ride over, however small, was left back with the ancient car.

Cain never left the lower quarters. She claimed the movement of the ship was not her style and kept to herself down where no one could see. I knew the sickness from losing the SoH was affecting her, and that the rotting parts of her skin were spreading. None of us knew how to help her, though, so we let her be.

Palls stayed outside at the head of the ship and never moved. Once or twice, I saw him fiddling with the bind collar he had brought along, but I didn't say anything.

I kept to myself in the rear. That's where I saw the land creep away so that's where I stayed. Meanwhile, D and Not-Mark stayed midship conversing. D had been shocked when he first saw the little blue streaker. Actually, I couldn't tell if it was shock or distrust, but it was definitely a rotten cocktail of both. Not-Mark never left his side, either because he wanted to or because it was an order.

After what felt like days of staring at the same grumbling ocean, I had enough. I marched right to where D was perched, intent on having it out with him. The two of us hadn't said a word to each other since I came on board and the silence was starting to suffocate me.

On my approach, D flashed a smile. Not-Mark was hunched over beside him and only managed to scowl at me as I got near.

"Aren't you cold?" I asked, pointing toward his dangling, naked nether-regions.

"No," replied the liar, but as he walked by I could literally hear his teeth chattering.

Grimacing, I turned back to D. "You sure we can trust him?"

Still within earshot, the blue man turned back to me. "For your information, I was set to spend my days trapped in a frozen lake until kingdom come. But then, I was set free."

"And who do we have to thank for that?" I replied sarcastically.

Not-Mark threw his gangly arms up. "Why does it matter?" Glancing back toward the ground, the little blue man shook his head. "Still, it calls. My hole. My rut. The frozen bite draws me back. But I will not go back. I deserve to be out. I deserve ... I deserve..." His voice trailed off as he turned and slouched away.

I sighed. "It's amazing how safe I feel with everyone here. Such an amazing team, we are."

"It's good to see you, too, Grey." D tucked his hands in his pockets. "Don't worry about him. I promised to set him free once he leads us back. The route he took here wasn't the normal one, so it should come in handy."

D's demeanor made me uneasy, and it didn't take me long to figure out why. The way D looked at me, his eyes soft and posture reserved, was the way two strangers interacted. To me, this could only mean one thing.

"You told me the last time we met that time works differently down here."

I went searching for something in D's eyes. Could he meet me halfway? Did I have to ask?

The demon that used to be my roommate dropped his head. "It's been a while, Grey. The last time we spoke, back in Limbo, right before we got this little traveling hellfire show on the road ... that was a long time ago."

My leg started to tremble. "How long?"

"I don't think—"

"I'm not asking you what you *think*. How long has it been?"

D looked out into the sea where the bodies were reaching swells of ten to twelve feet in height before spilling over onto themselves.

"It's going on seven years since I saw you last, Grey. Just about seven years since I walked out of that meeting room in the First Circle."

I had closed my eyes, hoping it would soften the blow. But the news still bit into me so violently that I felt I had dreamed everything up and my body was hanging limply out of the jaws of that canine, Fen. When I opened my eyes, only D was standing there—and he knew what I was going to ask next. He slowly shook his head and grabbed me just as I felt the wail blossoming in my chest. Like a hot bubble, the feeling burst out of my throat.

The next thing I knew, I was on the ground. D had caught me, but I was groaning louder than the Sea of Corpses.

I hadn't saved Petty in time.

Dad was gone.

D explained the circumstances.

Dad had felt sick one morning. Felt slow. Mom pushed him to see a doctor, as she always would. For once, he didn't give her lip—a sign he was just as worried. The docs ran tests and spotted it for what it was: a minor stroke.

His health corkscrewed shortly after and he was bedridden. Depression does this—it can amplify a sinus infection and make it feel like a full-blown flu. The whole body can't fight everything at once, especially if you're not emotionally sound. Losing both of his daughters in one night was the catalyst to all of this.

D told me that Dad fought extremely hard. He said he hadn't told either of my parents about fetching me and Petty from Hell, but it was like Dad could sense it. He never gave up, though he couldn't convince his body of the same thing. My mom was by his side the entire time.

"I constantly came down to check in and see if you got here, but you never showed," D began as part of an apology. Not wanting to hear it, I reached up and touched his lips. He stopped talking. After a long time of us huddled there, me leaning up against his chest, his legs forming barriers around me, D placed his chin on my head.

"Where do we go from here?"

It was a loaded question, one that was either attached to the two of us, or the ship and the fate of its crew. I only had the drive to answer one.

"My mom? How is she?"

D laughed. "Still kicking ass. She made this lasagna the other day that had five layers of cheese. A real shame the cooking gene skipped you completely." I gave him a soft shot in the ribs. D laughed again and added, "She misses him a lot. She misses all of you."

"Who are the Old Gods?" This was not how I had planned on asking, but my emotions were flushing out of me.

D, being D, answered reluctantly. "The Old Gods were here from the start. I'm talking way back—The Holy War. Every foul creature you can think of. When the Dark Lord fell, they became his generals and served as the architects of Hell." He paused. "I heard about the Furies. And I heard you killed Fen."

I sighed. "Who snitched?"

"The blue guy."

Finally, I pushed away from D and sat up on my own. "Any idea how I was able to blow up an eternal creature? I'm pretty sure that's nowhere in the 'So Now You're a Warden: User Manual'."

D shook his head. "The hierarchy in Hell has always been the same. The Wardens run the Circles, which were created by the Old Gods. After them, there's only the Dark Lord himself."

Recalling Hel's words, I had to ask. "What about dragons? Where do they fit in?"

D's confused face said it all. "Can't say I've seen or heard about dragons down here. Look, I don't believe you killed an actual Old God. That's just ... it's just not possible. Fenrir is a beast of the apocalypse, Grey, not some yappy dog someone forgot to curb. There's no way you could have

killed it. Now for the increase in your power … the only way I can make sense of it is that you must be getting close to your Circle. Wardens get stronger as they get closer to their worlds. This is mine and I hold dominion over it." D popped the collar on his pea coat and added, "Don't know if you were paying attention, but, uh, I made this here ship with my will alone."

A curl of wind picked up and slammed into the side of the ship, causing one side of the vessel to rupture as rain splintered wood out into the sea of bodies. From out of the hole it left behind, I spotted Cain, still sick and half asleep, climb out of her bed, shuffle over to the only open window the implosion left behind, shut it with one hand, and flop back onto the mattress.

"Four stars for craftsmanship!" I gave D a slow clap and felt dirty for it. "So, I'm getting closer to my Circle. Does that mean I'll be able to decapitate demons, or create a reality show that doesn't seem exploitative of another human being's suffering?"

"You'll get stronger the closer you get to yours, but don't get cocky," he warned. "An Old God can come and pluck my eyes out in a hiccup if I look at them wrong. Even here."

"Sure," I replied, but not because I believed what he was saying. He wasn't on Hel's show with me. I still remembered that beast leaping at me. I remembered thinking it was all over and then, just a snap later, its fur disintegrating in midair, the cry it let out … Hel screaming and tearing at herself in grief. I had done the impossible and the fact even D couldn't explain it scared the hell out of me.

The two of us stood, and D leaned against the banister. "I didn't know how to tell you about your father. He was … he was a great man."

"It's fine." And in truth, it was. I knew I couldn't hang on to that grief. I had made a decision. I decided to come down to get Petty instead of going up to see him one last time. I knew I had to carry the weight of that with me for as long as I existed. But I realized it didn't mean going to see him would have been the "right" choice. Dad was going to leave, whether I was there or not, and then it would be just Mom and me, mourning that half of our family that had been taken from us.

A dull worry set in. Sure, my mom was still alive and the city was in one piece. But by this time, my mom had already set into her mind that her two

girls had been dead for almost ten years. Is that something I could go back to? I only had four more floors to go. I was so close, but time was not on my side.

"There's no turning back now. I know it. We made it this far." I ran my fingers through my hair and took a deep breath. Sliding next to D on the banister, I asked, "And what about you? How far are you coming along with me this time, D?"

Carefully bumping his shoulder against mine, the demon replied, "Well, you know. I figured we already survived one apocalypse together. Might as well see this one to the end, too. I mean, we make a great team."

"I *died* the last time we teamed up," I corrected. "At best, we're hovering around an F to F+."

D snickered. "I'll take it."

There wasn't a lot to say after this. There was just us, the dark sky, and the large waves of bodies thumping against the ship's hull. I know it sounds strange, but I liked having D there. Even if he wasn't saying anything. I enjoyed knowing he was close by. And I honestly felt like we both would have been content staying right there—silent but in each others' orbit— until we crashed the damned ship right into Satan's crotch.

Of course, that's not what happened.

"Screech!" Palls yelled as he came running to where we stood. He pointed to the sky and there it was, flapping its oversized wings as it managed the wind. It made two turns over us and then plummeted down to land just a few feet from where we stood. Even Cain and Not-Mark came up to see it.

Opening its beak slowly, the distorted voice came spilling out again. This time, not only did it know whom to address, its message was only three words long.

"COME GET HER."

I pushed D aside and stepped to where the creature could both see me and hear the three words I wanted it to understand.

"ON MY WAY."

I flicked my fingers and snapped at the same time, causing long sparks to leap onto the creature and set it ablaze. The five of us just watched in silence as the monster bird burned, withered, and entered non-existence.

D AND I met to strategize. According to him, the Six and Seventh Circles were going to be problematic.

"The Furies are sisters who rule the lower City, Pandemonium. Just imagine the inverse of New Necro and you'll start to understand what I'm about to tell you. It's a city of demons—pure ones. The worst of the worst. The air down there is thick, the hellfire is as pure as it gets, and there's nowhere to go if we get overrun. That's not counting the Furies themselves." Choosing his words carefully, D added, "Now, I know you're not going to like this too much, but it's the truth. We're going to need all hands on deck if we're going to survive that place."

When I looked up, I followed his sightline to the man at the front of the ship.

Begrudgingly, I pushed away from my post and leaned back into my twisted ostrich pose. As the strain on my body lessened, D asked, "All good, Grey?"

I stood up straight. "All good."

As I dragged my feet toward Gaffrey Palls, my ex-roommate called after me.

"Be gentle."

Palls sensed me as I got close and quickly brought the collar of his coat closer to his face. It didn't take a genius to figure out what he was up to standing there all by himself. The old me would have just blurted out what I wanted to ask to get it over with. It would have been brutal, but clean.

Apparently, that wasn't my style anymore.

Palls spoke without turning around. "Looks like you got the hang of that hellfire. Ain't got nothing else to teach you, lady. Unless you came for another reason."

"Yeah, Palls. I came here for a chit-chat about as much as you're up here for the view," I replied as a twelve-foot surge of gray bodies rolled nearby.

When I got around to see his face, Palls' cheeks were drawn. Only his eyes stood out in the low light. This is where I would have typically walked away. I didn't stick my nose into anyone's problems and Palls didn't want to talk—that much was obvious—but I had to say something first.

"I'm not an idiot, Palls. I'm hard-headed, but not an idiot."

"You're also violent, temperamental, emotionally distant, vengeful..." Palls glanced over. "I'm naming your good traits, Grey, so don't pull yourself into knots about it. Just finish what you have to say."

"As much as I hate your guts, I'm not going to ignore the fact I wouldn't have made it this far without you. If you weren't there from the beginning, Mason would have carved me up into cold cuts a million times by now."

"Your point?" Catching himself, Palls shook his head. "I mean, it's fine. You can go back to hating me once this is all over, if it suits you."

I sighed. "You know, I've never heard you curse. Not once."

"Is that so?"

"Yeah, and it's fucking infuriating."

This made him laugh, but his eyes left the reality we were in. He slumped over and I caught him. Pulling back his coat collar showed the runes on the Bind were turning on, one by one.

Using some leverage, I dug under the metal with my fingers and pried the collar off his neck with a violent jerk that also—and totally by accident—slammed him headfirst into the banister.

"Ow!" Groggily, Palls rolled over as I dangled the device right in front of his eyes.

"This isn't going to help."

For the first time, I saw anger rise in Pall's face. "Save the sermon. You leapt into one of my memories and you think you know anything? You don't, okay? You don't know me."

"Oh yeah?" I shot back, "so who's Mel?"

I knew I shouldn't cross that line, but I did and regretted it instantly.

Palls' entire demeanor changed. I watched his hands in case he lashed out at me, but he just brought one to his face and did his best to hide behind it. "Who told you that name?"

"You called her name out in the memory."

Palls snatched the Bind from my hand, but instead of bashing me with it, slammed it to the ground. Just when I thought this killed our conversation, Palls exhaled slowly.

"She was my sister. She...." Shaking his head, he turned his back to me. "If you really must know, that memory you saw was just the beginning of the nightmare I've been living for almost seventy-five years. That's what that thing did to me. It kept me alive while rotting away at me from the inside. Soon as I got back from the war, Mel was the one who took care of me. Mom was gone and my father, well, let's just say he was as good as dead. So Mel picked up the pieces. Not uncommon for guys to come back from the war with more than a few screws loose. But of course, I also had that thing in me."

Picking the device up, Palls looked down at the Bind in his hand.

I kept my distance, but knew I needed to ask, "What happened to her, Gaffrey?"

The large man picked himself up and stared out across the Sea of the Corpses.

"She was afraid of what was inside me. Don't think she knew exactly what it was, but she could sense it. Mel was always good for that. The problem was the Shade was out to corrupt me, completely. It saw Mel as a threat."

"A threat?" My mind started to spin. I didn't like where this was going.

"Shades are going to corrupt your soul; there's no way to fight it. But they can't if you're connected to people. Not fully. They need you alone. In a dark place inside your own head. That's the soldier the Shade found on that battlefield. It found me alone and took advantage."

And that was it. The Shade that had taken over my body as a child had made two big mistakes. First, it didn't think I could have been pre-packaged with my own anxieties and self-doubt. But also, the support system I had from birth—Mom and Dad and Petty; Hell, even Pops and Lady and Donaldson the Legendary Boy Scout—had added to clamping down on the Shade throughout my short life. I had been saved, not just by my will alone, but by the people who were there to support me.

Palls sat back down and drew his legs close to his chest, quite a sight for a guy his size, and buried his head into his knees. He was emotional, breathing hard.

"I lost her, Grey. I lost my sister."

His words sunk into my skin like nails. It was if his pain had leapt into me. Part of me wanted to back away and run, but the other part was drowning. My jaw was locked and my entire body felt clenched like it was caught in mid-seizure. Fighting through all of this, I managed to say, "It wasn't your fault, Palls. It was the Shade."

"I couldn't protect her." Enraged, Palls let both his arms go up in black hellfire, but the flames were small compared to when I first saw them, and that could only mean one thing: as a Warden, Gaffrey Palls was too far from his Circle to mean much anymore. Noticing this as well, he let the dark tongues extinguish and re-covered his face with his hands.

"That thing kept me alive this entire time. By the time I stepped into your apartment, I was gone, a shell of a human being. You've seen them rot away at people before?"

"Yeah." Not that I wanted to remember them, but all the Shades had warped the minds and bodies of the people they had taken over. Almost instantly.

"Shades feed on your vices," Palls explained. "They bastardize and mutate your body. The Shade in me kept me alive to consume the others—a power play. But even when my body was no longer mine, I never

gave up hope. You asked why I was coming down here with you? The truth is that I know a thing or two about losing a little sister. But also, I wanted to look for her myself. I wanted to make sure she didn't end up down here because of me."

I sighed. "And there's no sign of her?"

"None." Palls turned the metal collar in his hand, again and again. "And I guess I should be happy about that, but part of me just wants to see her again, you know?" Finding a smile, Palls added, "Guess I can't have both."

I leaned back against the railing. "You don't need to keep reliving that pain. Now—and I can't believe I'm actually saying this—but I'm starting to realize that maybe dying and ending up in Hell is the perfect way to restart your life."

Palls scoffed but I didn't let him off the hook yet.

"So you fucked up. Who hasn't? I mean, sure, our two fuck ups led to the sort-of-end of the world. So what? You've fought for your sister. You've looked for her. You've risked everything. And if she's not down here, what will you do next? Life doesn't end, even in the afterlife."

Palls took a moment to sit with what I said, and in many ways so did I. Was this the same ideal I was chasing? Was I really able to shake off the chains of the old Grey—the ultimate fuckup? Could I save my sister?

Palls held up the collar as the three runes turned off one by one by one. "You know, you kind of remind me of her. Loudmouth. Hot-headed."

"Well then I hope I never meet her," I replied honestly.

The man grunted an approval. Before he walked away, Palls launched the Bind as far as he could and it vanished behind a swell of bodies.

I watched him leave and felt odd about the whole conversation. It all had been so fast I couldn't believe what had happened. The walls built between Palls and I had just caved in, and for the first time, we saw each other as the people we once were—or at least the people we could have been if our lives hadn't been wrecked by Shades. I can't say I ever imagined giving Gaffrey Palls a pep talk, let alone one that helped me deal with my anxieties as well. I guess the afterlife makes people do crazy things.

I spoke into the open air and turned back to the sea. "Things could be worse."

"It sure can be," a sing-songy voice replied out of nowhere and I nearly fell over myself in my attempts to get away.

Standing in the air not five feet from the edge of our ship was a familiar threat. She wore the same oversized black coat I had seen her in before. Her purple hair waved back and forth as if caught in an invisible stream.

The Fury unzipped the coat she was wearing and let it fall onto the bodies below. She must have been eight feet tall. Her face was flat and snake-like with yellow diamond patterns on her cheek. She wore a feathered boa and black thigh high boots. Her body was made of layered golden scales that made her hide look more like armor than flesh.

She reached out with her black claws and hissed. "Time to go, Amanda Grey."

As she spoke, a forked tongue at least a foot long hung down around her chest.

The others came running, Palls leading the charge, but the Fury looked unimpressed.

A fiery chain flew from the back end of the ship and bound itself around the Fury's neck. She let out a faint "Erk" and drifted to the side. Tracing the chain back, I could see red ember binds shooting from D's hands. Glowing with dark energy, he began reeling in the flying Fury closer to the ship.

"You're up, Palls!"

"Got her!"

With a hefty shoulder charge, Gaffrey Palls busted down the railing and cleared the gap to where the Fury floated. But, even bound, she took a step forward and spun in place, the back of her elbow connecting with him so hard it caused sparks to fly. The blow knocked him out of the air and sent him crashing into one of the masts.

As she reached up to free herself from the chains, she began screaming, "It burns! It burns!" But then, with an expression of pure boredom, the creature flicked at the chain and it snapped like cheap tape as she added, "or not."

Hovering closer to my face, the Fury smiled, revealing four rows of sharp teeth. “I would say to come with me and I would let everyone live, but I have absolutely zero intention of living up to that promise.”

She gestured slowly to the ocean and the sea of bodies stopped swaying. One by one, the corpses stood, turned to face the ship, and began stacking themselves against the sides as they began climbing up the ship by the thousands.

In an instant, the corpses were on board, shambling toward us. So many boarded us in such a short time that the ship broke in half under their weight. The back end snapped off and rolled backward, leaving the front end tumbling with all of us trying to find our footing.

Just as I turned to blast away the incoming horde, something struck me in the throat and I collapsed. The Fury laughed as she grabbed me by the wrist and took flight.

“Offffff-weeeeee-goooooooo,” she sang as a fiery portal opened above our heads. We flew toward it in a flash. This, coupled with the fact one of my hands was caught in her grasp and the other was busy nursing the neck she almost broke, left me with no options to fight back.

I felt my stomach seize up. Like I had downed too many drinks, my abdominal muscles contracted all at once. My lungs and hips suddenly became heavy with a pressure that felt like I had swallowed a bowling ball for dinner. It felt like said bowling ball was rising up, crushing my guts, stuffing itself up my sore throat.

Without warning, a thick stream of black fire flew from my lips. It splattered out some fifty feet as I did my very best impression of a human blowtorch. Laced with a bevy of projectile vomit lava chunks, the flames caught the Fury’s legs and torso and she went up like kindling.

The Fury howled and we both fell about twenty feet right onto the tilting ship. I landed hard on my side, but at least it was one big splat. The Fury hit one of the masts, corkscrewed, and then smashed the banister with her head as she fell.

I coughed and ash rose like ghosts from my tongue, but the fire from my stomach went out. I couldn’t see anyone. Cain, Palls, D—I couldn’t be sure if they were still fighting somewhere on the ship or if the dead had already torn them apart.

Nearby, the Old God screamed as the black flames ate away at her slowly. She was now just a torso without a lower half, yet she was still coming for me, using her claws to drag herself in my direction.

"I cannot … dieee …" Her eyes were wide with panic and hatred. Her waving hair was a swaying bonfire now. Then, after muttering one single word, her entire body blackened into dust.

Her last word stayed with me as the entire ship, bursting at the seams with naked flesh, finally buckled under the weight of the corpses and we were all pitched overboard.

The Fury had called me a Dragon.

THE NEXT THING I knew, I opened my eyes and saw nothing but a black hole painted into a perfect gray backdrop. From out of this perfect circle, three voices bickered.

"Is she dead," asked voice one.

"Everything here is dead," replied voice two sarcastically.

Voice three barked at the one who came before her. "I believe she wasn't asking for your philosophical bullshit. Is she dead or not?"

"How am I supposed to know? Should I check for a pulse? Breathing?"

There was a clatter and one voice let out a hearty, "Ah-ha!"

"Ah-ha!" the other two rejoined.

There was a long pause and then a black bird-like claw came into view and hovered some five feet from my face. As soon as it opened, a stone struck me right on my forehead.

Jolting up, I screamed and cursed, trying to grab the nearest person to punch the hell out of them. What I found instead was a thickly pleated dress that looked made of shiny black feathers. There was gold trim around the wrists and shoulders, giving the wearer of the dress an air of nobility.

The illusion was lost when I saw the thing wearing it had the head of a crow.

"Look at that. You're not dead. Someone cut a cake," she cooed to the other two crow ladies standing behind her and then hobbled off at an extremely slow pace.

The black hole was not a hole at all, but a sun of pure darkness burning in the cloudless sky overhead. There was nothing around me for miles in every direction. No ship. No bodies. No Furies and no friends. Only three crow ladies hoisting tiny baskets in the crooks of their thin arms. The land was flat and barren in every direction, with endless drought as far as the eye could see.

"Are you coming or what?" one of them shouted at me.

I had no idea how to answer, so I just got up and followed.

The three crow crones walked. Okay, maybe calling it "walking" was generous. The steps they took underneath their long dresses were so slow I could have run fourteen figure eights around them before the three of them completed a yard. They marched at least four feet apart from each other at all times, but always in a single file. I walked behind them, but their choppy pace was agonizing. While it was painstaking to travel that slow, the three of them had absolutely nothing to say, making the trek feel like someone was slowly removing a splinter over the course of a week.

The major problem was there didn't seem to be a destination. Or a point, a reason, a fate, a foreseeable lunch break ... nothing! Just teeny steps, black rocks in baskets, and emptiness.

Finally, after what felt like ages, one of the crow crones stopped and faced me. She cocked her head to one side and then the next. Then she exclaimed, "Oh, you're still here?"

It took every ounce of my being not to snap my fingers at her. Instead, I slapped my hand down and pinned it to my leg. "You... you told me to—"

"Hold this," she demanded and thrust her basket into my hand. The weight of it nearly broke me in half as I keeled over and hit the ground. This tiny wicker basket with its five or six little black stones had made a soft crater around it in the dirt and was nearly impossible to pick up.

Dusting myself off, the crow crone bobbed her head from side to side as if looking for something. The other three had done the same. Cupping a hand over my eyes, I took a good look around. I couldn't see or hear anything, and from what I could tell, the dark sun hadn't moved from its position above us this entire journey.

"Where are we headed?"

The other two crows crones looked back when I spoke. "You're still here?"

"We should keep moving if we're going to make it on time," the closest one to me commanded.

"Make it where?" I asked.

Annoyed, she scooped up the basket as easily as if it weighed nothing and threw it onto her arm. "We're headed to Pandaemonium, of course."

The pace we were traveling turned into a hurried one. There was still a barren wasteland and still a freakish sun, but the crones moved diligently. Still in single file, but now at a faster pace than before.

Ever so often, we would see a stranger walking toward us. The figure would be a skeleton dressed in ragged clothing, carrying a slab on their back that I quickly recognized was a tombstone. Most would pass us without acknowledging we were there, but there were a few times these strangers dropped to their knees and began to dig with their bony hands. After setting their tombstones, they would climb into the hole and drag the dirt over them. Sometimes, rather than going in, we would come across a grave freshly made and watch as a stranger pulled themselves out.

"What are they doing?" I asked of one of the crow crones.

"The souls here cannot cease looking for their end," one told me. "This is the Sixth Circle: the body of unrest. Here, souls who were fascinated with their own deaths come to suffer. Here, those who have committed heresy cannot rest until they find their specific resting place and bury themselves. Only one grave, only one soul. If eternity it takes to find rest, then eternity it will take."

"One section?" I looked around. This Circle seemed even larger than Abaddon. At least there were things to look at while I was there. I cast away the thought of these lost souls and asked a question I should have asked from the beginning.

"Hey! Did any of you see anyone where you found me? A man, a demon, an angel, and a liar were all riding a boat—"

"I hate jokes like that," one crone sneered.

"I know that one. They were all dead in the end," insisted another.

I sighed and dropped the subject. I wasn't sure what could have happened to my friends and hated thinking about the worst. Could they have gone to the city without me?

"You are headed to Pandemonium?" I asked.

"That's what I said," the crone squawked.

"Why? What's there?"

The crone held up her basket. "We're building a wall."

I nodded. "What's the new wall supposed to do?"
"No one said anything about a 'new' wall," the crone ahead of her replied. "The wall we're building is there. Has always been there."

"So you're rebuilding? I'm confused."

"Of course you are. You're still talking," crone number one shouted back at us. "Look, the wall we are building is there and belongs there so we are making it there so it can stay there and always be there."

"Got it," I said, lying. "Pandaemonium. I kinda need to get through it. Do you know anything about the place that can help?"

"The city of Pandaemonium was not its original name, just like the city of New Necropolis is not its name either."

"People have forgotten it. They forget everything."

"The two cities were called The City of Dis and the City of Dae."

"The Old Gods created them to be what was known as 'Pendulum Cities' because they are the balance on which Hell is built on. All manner of beasts and demons wait for you there. They are mirrors of each other."

I literally tripped over myself. "The Old Gods created them? Do you know anything about the Old Gods?"

"Everyone knows the Old Gods, though I'm sure they get talked about less and less up in the higher Circles," crone number two declared. "But that's how hearsay goes. Things happen last year, it's history. Things happen last century, it's myth."

There was something decidedly odd about the way the crones spoke.

I had originally pegged them as your average weirdo-denizens of Hell, but there were times they slipped into an area that made me question who I had been traveling with the whole time. How innocent were these things, really?

Feeling like I would lose nothing by pushing my luck, I threw them a comment to see how they would react. "All I know about the Old Gods is they served as architects here in Hell."

One of the crones puffed her feathers. "Heh. Old Gods? Served? They served nothing but themselves. From the moment the Dark Lord held dominion here, they were dying to exact their own powers. Their arrogance. Their dark hearts."

"Stupid creatures with stupid mouths," one crone waxed. "They were his generals during his war with God, but they all became arrogant. They wanted a war here in Hell to decide who rules. They secretly planned to overthrow the ruler. That's why the Dark Lord created the only thing that could keep them in check."

I scratched my head. "He created something that could beat the Old Gods?"

"Of course he did. See at first, there was the Beast."

"Vicious creature. Seven heads. Really bad smell."

"Awful smell," crone three agreed. "But the Dark Lord had another idea."

"He did. Another plan to keep the Old Gods in check," crone one chuckled.

"Yes. With his bare hands, he tore the seven-headed beast into seven dragons..."

"...and gave them dominion over the first Seven Circles of Hell."

"Seven dragons?" Remembering the dying Fury's words, I had to ask, "What happened to the dragons? Are they still around?"

At first, the crones didn't seem like they were going to answer and I thought I had overstepped my questions, when one finally spoke, enunciating carefully so I could hear the capitalization in her words. "The Dark Lord vanished shortly after creating the Dragons. And so there was a war—a war between the Old Gods and the Dragons for rights to Hell itself."

"And who won?"

"The Old Gods found a way. If they couldn't kill the Dragons, and they couldn't beat the Dragons, then they would get rid of them. So, using one of their powers of transformation, they banished the Dragons into the world of the living. They stripped them of their memories and powers, and in the world of Man, the Dragons found themselves transformed into—"

"Crows," I finished as the answer hit me like a brick. It couldn't be a coincidence. It wasn't. The Shades I had fought off on Earth were actually the Seven Dragons of Hell. That's the connection: Shades, Wardens, and the Dragons were the same thing. While it made sense, I could feel something was missing. "But weren't the Shades connected to the end of the world prophecy? The last chapter stuff?"

The crone next to me shook her head. "Just because the world ends doesn't mean the story does," she snickered. "The Dark Lord's disappearance and his return now, the movement of the Old Gods, the return of the Dragons. There have even been whispers of Heaven being turned inside out." The crone held up one clawed finger and added, "This could mean the end of everything, the end for us all. But then what?"

"We've arrived," announced the crone furthest from me. We hadn't taken many steps in any direction, but sure enough, piercing the horizon was a castle appearing like a black shard sprouting from the ground. As we walked toward this object, more of it came into view. The fortress sported four gnarled towers, each one rising from the sharp edges of vine-covered walls like the writhing legs of an overturned insect. When we arrived, an immense metal gate greeted us. It must have stood fifty to seventy feet high and its bars were made of rusted metal thicker than my body.

The crones led me to one of the walls just to the right of the gate. Then, one by one, they dumped the contents of their baskets at its base. The rocks clattered to the ground and, seeing their job done, the three crow crones turned around and started walking back in the direction we had come.

I dashed in front of them. "Wait! Stop! Nope! We walked all the way here. It's been miles."

"Maybe," responded one crone.

"Days?" I asked.

"Eh," answered another.

"Fine. It's been a really freakin' long time and we've spent it walking. Endlessly. And now you just want to throw your stupid little stones down and walk back? For what?"

"To get more stones," the trio replied in unison. I'd never been given a "Duh! What the fuck is wrong with you" look from a bird, but I definitely got one now. I felt like an idiot as they started walking away.

I heard a sound that I first thought was thunder. The vibrations rattled beneath our feet and rolled along the plains. A pattern expanded on the initial boom, and I traced the sound not into the sky, but behind the walls of the castle. Drums. Loud, pounding drums.

After the echoes finally died away, two figures stepped out onto the edge of the wall.

The shortest Fury pointed down at me and hollered, "Welcome, Amanda Grey. I knew you'd show up here, eventually."

The Furies were still wearing the heavy black coat with the high collar, so one had to stoop to take a closer look at my travel companions. "Still carrying those stones, eh? Our building days are over, Morrigan."

Beside me, the three crow crones started to vibrate as they shuttered together into one body. When the feathers settled, she called back to the Fury. "Meg. Alec. I want to say it's been a few centuries since we last spoke, but that would imply I missed you in some kind of way."

The whole conversation floored me. The crones—no, *crone*—was an Old God?

"Grey belongs to us," the taller Fury demanded. "Are you going to object?"

"I'm only here to drop off my stones to fix that wall," Morrigan said, pointing to the wall that obviously didn't need fixing.

The Fury gestured to a servant I couldn't see and they both retreated. Shortly after, there was a large creak, followed by a grinding of gears as the gates leading to the City of Dis slowly began to rise.

"You were one of them this entire time," I called over to Morrigan.

She leaned in close and blinked her black eyes at me. "We are what we are, Grey. The question is, what will you be when you enter the City of Dis? What will you be when you leave?"

She turned and made to leave.

"You were the one who changed the Dragons into crows, weren't you?" I asked.

Her clawed hand made a swirl in the air and returned to her side as she vanished.

As the gate reached its highest position and locked into place, I knew I had a serious fight on my hands. Watching the two Furies step out of the colossal opening to meet me, I had no plan to stop them from tearing me to pieces. Four of me could fit inside the broadest one's coat and the tall one stood at least fifteen feet tall. Of course, there was also the fact that I was a Dragon— the mortal enemy of the Old Gods—*and* that I had incinerated one of their sisters (which, I felt, was frowned upon in most social circles).

Preparing myself for a fight, the Furies stared me down.

Then each took a knee.

Bowing her head, the shortest Fury told me,

"Welcome to your kingdom, Lady Grey."

THE WALK INTO the city was a dizzying one. Beyond the gates, the world was entirely different. The black sun could not be seen in the sky, which was then replaced by dark clouds that moved and curled about in a bright red soup. Ash constantly fell from above, making the air particularly uncomfortable to wade through. I couldn't breathe the way I did when I was alive, but the aura here was definitely smothering my chest and lips.

Around us, workers climbed up and down through the many levels of the outlying castle. These workers were all dark marionettes, like the servants in Olive Garden—like Petty once was. Seeing them and thinking about my little sister as one of these creatures forced me to keep my discomfort in check, especially in front of my escort.

The Furies said nothing as we moved through room after room. In every space, I got the sense I was centuries late to a party. The wooden tables were falling to dust; the walls were crumbling or non-existent. There were a few art pieces strung about, but the canvases were ripped or eaten through. I felt as if I was walking through the ruin of a civilization a few hundred lifetimes after its ruin.

"Where are you taking me?" I did my best to sound in charge, but I got the sense I needed to tread carefully. The tall one was still the freakier one of the two as her coat moved and jostled around from time to time and I heard the whispers of small voices. The broader one moved with lumbering steps, but I felt she could turn on me in an instant.

As we walked through a room with a high, arching ceiling and seven pillars of broken marble, I couldn't help feel overwhelmed by how desolate and empty this Circle of Hell was. The room's black floor tiles were missing and even more broken furniture was strewn about. The only thing that looked even remotely worth seeing was a tapestry hanging by the back wall.

As if on a hideous tour, the tall Fury called back to me, "This is the Old City—the remnants of what Hell used to be. Back when it was all 'brimstone and pitchforks.' We're escorting you, Lady Grey, to where you will rule."

I laughed nervously. "'Lady Grey.' Why do you keep calling me that?"

As we walked by it, I couldn't help but pause at the tapestry. It must have been ten feet long in every direction and made of red satin. Its edges were tattered and uneven which made the entire cloth look ancient. There were figures woven in poses surrounding a black throne— beasts from every nightmare that you can imagine: Medusa, giants, Cyclopes, massive spiders, hellhounds, floating eyeballs, a muscular unicorn in a leotard. Mixed in were versions of the Furies. Even Hel and Fenrir were painted into the bottom right corner.

A horned demon with fiery eyes sat on the throne and above its head, a dragon with seven heads spouting fire stood between it and the other creatures.

"What is this?"

"A prophecy, spun before the start of Time itself," the Fury responded. "This is the oldest relic of Lower Hell. The first dark testament that can be remembered."

I found myself staring at the Beast, taking note of the smoke billowing from its nostrils and the seven crowns on its seven heads.

While I was distracted, the shorter Fury drew a small dagger and, in one blinding movement, slashed me across the shoulder.

Grabbing the wound, I dropped back and prepared for the next attack. But it never came.

The Fury set the weapon back on her belt and covered herself again.

A steady heat rose from beneath the gaps in my fingers as the pain spread from my shoulder to my chest. Instead of blood, pouring out of the slash on my shoulder were large blades of black fire. From this, I found my entire body became encased in dark flames.

When the hideous gash on my shoulder closed itself, and the pain in my body disappeared, a gown—another damned dress!—of black fire spread around me, one with long, draping sleeves and a hood that covered my head. Seven fiery tails sprouted from the hood and lashed against the ground behind me. Instead of burning my skin, I felt power rising within me. I couldn't control it, but I didn't need to.

"What did you do to me?" I cried, looking down at this flaming garb.

"You are home, Lady Grey," the tall Fury laughed. "This is what the power of a Dragon can do. But not just any Dragon. Before you test your power, I suggest being careful not to—"

Whatever advice she was trying to give me, I didn't exactly wait for it to land before I gave my fingers a snap. With the size and velocity of a cannonball, a flaming white sphere flew from my hand and into the tapestry itself, lighting the entire cloth up like kindling.

I immediately started apologizing. "Sorry, I—"

The tapestry fell into ash, revealing I had fired a hole into the wall behind it as well.

"That's on me!"

In the distance, another wall exploded.

"That one, too."

And the next.

"Oh, c'mon!"

When the loud crashes finally subsided, and the dust had settled, we were all able to look through the hole and follow a clear path of destruction right until the outer wall. The blast had annihilated the entire south side of the castle, leaving behind a giant cloud of burning debris open to the vast wasteland

The two Furies silently looked at each other and then back at me.

"Right, well." I cleared my throat. "Lead on!"

As we left this room, I seemed to be the only one to notice that just beyond the smoldering rubble, which used to be the castle's outer wall, sat Morrigan's stones piled neatly as could be.

Next, we arrived in a circular room with a round platform at its center. Unlike the others, this chamber was expertly made with gold carvings and white walls. The high arches of this space reminded me of a church, which creeped me out completely.

Both Furies boarded the platform and I followed their lead. A marionette came and pulled a lever on the side of the wall, causing the platform to come to life with a sputter. We began to descend.

There was a brief moment of darkness, broken up the soft pops and crackles coming off of my robe.

Standing so close to the Furies, I figured if I really needed to, I could let out one big blast that could take us all out on this platform. I felt one of them open her coat and draw her limb out of the sleeve and, remembering her last attack on me, I jumped back instantly. The Fury pointed a clawed finger at the City in front of us.

"Welcome to Pandemonium, Lady Grey."

Pandemonium, or what Morrigan said was once called the City of Dis, was exactly like New Necro, only it was a metropolis growing upside-down out of the ceiling instead. In fact, at one point, the elevator we rode in flipped on a set axis, spinning us upside-down, or right-side-up according to how Dis was positioned. Though this made me feel dizzy at first, I quickly acclimated to the new perspective.

The City was really as the old crow crone had said: Dis and Dae were pendulum cities and mirrors of each other. It was still a civilization built into the darkness of a cave, just like its sister city. There were skyscrapers and buildings, red lights forming a single line of traffic up the main streets, smaller buildings hiding out on the outskirts of the town like scattered crumbs. There was even a black skyscraper jutting up from the center, just like in New Necro.

I will say where I found the adverts and commercials in New Necro unsettling, Pandemonium took all of them to another horrific level. There were ads for as far as the eye could see. Too many ads, in fact. I would say there were at least three signs for every building in Dis which just made the place look more like a metropolis someone had decorated with cut-up sales circulars and annoying internet ads.

I watched as a small bi-plane dragged by an advert that read "ADOPT A PET FOR YOUR NEXT SACRIFICE" in big bold lettering (and Lobster font, of course) before crashing into a massive pop-up ad that appeared in the air before it and then spiral into the City as a twisting fireball.

Dis even had its own Maw, which I could spot due to the flocks of Screech's flowing out of its darkness. I noticed the flocks never entered the city and instead flew past us on their way to spread their poison to the surface.

We disembarked the elevator and the air here was even worse. It felt like something was kneeling on my back—like gravity was tearing the soul out of me. As if this didn't bother them at all, the two Furies removed their coats and inhaled slowly.

The shorter Fury stretched her toned arms and let out a yawn. She had two sets of wings—two black, two white—that spread like an unholy x on her back. Beneath her coat, she wore light pearl-colored lace with gold trim that flowed over her pale skin. A set of horns curved up from her temples and ended in black points. Her eyes were egg-white surrounded in deep pits of jet-black ink. Her lips were also black and sported hideous scars running up from the edges of her mouth like a smile carved by a blade. Aside from this and her limp black hair, her face was human-like, flawless. If it weren't for the fact the bitch had already tried to slice me into pieces, I would almost call her beautiful.

The tall Fury wasn't any easier to look at. Dropping her drape to the floor, I knew instantly why her coat moved on her own. Her body was skeletal, almost tree-like. Her face was a rounded skull whose mouth was in a permanent toothless smile. She had ragged brown hair that dropped all the way to the ground like a nest of weeds. Small creatures hung and played around the insides of her limbs. They were childlike, with tiny naked bodies, and wore masks with drawings on them—the kind you would find on the walls of a daycare—just with spectacularly macabre images. One mask was of a magical castle pouring hot oil on an invading army. Another was of a unicorn sodomizing an elf. The little demons giggled. They whispered. Some of them played tag in her rib cage. Another was snoozing in the scoop of her collarbone.

Of all the creatures I had come across in Hell, the Furies genuinely made me fear for my life. There's no way to sugarcoat this. It was obvious they could have, and should have, scattered my body parts to the wind at the gates of Dis. They were wary of something and I was sure it wasn't my pro-cooking skills.

I'll admit that, while terrifying, I came to be grateful for the Furies' monstrous looks. The City of Dis was crawling with demons of every kind. Spiders, lizards, harpies, seals. I'm going to come out and say this without wanting to go into specifics, but demon seals are the worst demons imaginable. The tusks and whiskers ... that honking noise.

The demons themselves lined the streets as we made our way to the central building in Pandemonium. I walked down the street, flanked by the two Old Gods, as every demon in the City peered at me with their glowing eyes from the sidewalks, windows, fire escapes, and manholes.

"We have planned for your arrival, Lady Grey," Alec, the tall Fury with the creepy children, whispered as if it were a secret. "The citizens have thrown you a welcoming parade."

I never went to a New York City parade. Too many people, too many barricades, too many bagpipes. Even though I didn't have experience to draw from, I was pretty sure it was not common practice for parade-goers to be shouting for you to be decapitated while going into graphic detail about what they want to do with your skull afterward.

One brave demon tried to leap out at me, but Meg, the multi-winged Fury, drew and threw one of her daggers in one sick movement that caught the crazed creature right between its bugged eyes. Caught in mid-air, the demon collapsed at my feet. Meg pulled the knife from its corpse, flicked its black blood into the crowd, and sheathed her weapon.

The walk reminded me of what Palls had told me about New Necro and how its citizens were not evil. I couldn't quite wrap my mind about it then, but it made sense walking around Dis. I guess standing in the middle of an entire city as over a million demons call to have your flesh ripped off really brings clarity to all of the questions in the universe.

The building at the center of the City looked just like the black spire in New Necro. Up close, the angular shape of its construction confused the hell of out me. There were impossible shapes holding up the entire one hundred-story building. I couldn't even be sure what the structure was made out of: stone, concrete, glass, or metal. It was the oddest thing I had ever seen, one that both radiated light and swallowed it.

We entered through the front doors and stood in a room of mirrors.

Behind this, two round doors rolled apart and let us through. The next room was white and, actually, quite beautiful. There were hanging plants, a grotto with a small waterfall. The walls were all white and the most amazing throne sat at the end on an elevated platform—one with seven spires rising from the top.

The Furies gestured for me to take my time inspecting the throne as they stood at the bottom patiently. Passing my hand over it, the throne felt cool to the touch and my burning mantle seemed to surge with power as I kept my fingers on its surface. I had never seen anything like the white and gold trim that formed its shell.

"So, this is my throne?"

"It is," Meg responded. Alec had plucked out one of her ribs and was using it as a rattle to entertain her kids.

"I'm going to address the elephant in the room," I started boldly. "I killed your sister and you're offering me a throne. It's not that I'm not grateful or anything. It's a nice throne. I'm just wondering why you're not a little more, oh I dunno, pissed about it?"

Meg flexed her neck, which made me see I'd hit a nerve. Still, she replied, "Tis was overzealous. Our sister got what she deserved." And then she added, "Blood under the bridge."

"Water," I corrected.

But Meg shook her head. "She was filled with water? That's pretty gross."

"You know there's this principle New Yorkers take to heart. 'When things are too good to be true, it usually means they are.' It's like when a train car pulls into the station and you see it's empty; that there are seats open for anyone with an ass. Tourists line up in front of the doors just to pile themselves in, but not a real New Yorker. You see, even before the train stops, real New Yorkers go find another car. We know an empty train car means the seats are coated in bodily discharge, or there is a gang of roaches having a knife fight inside."

Confused, the two Furies glanced at each other.

"Lady Grey?"

"I'm saying you'll have to excuse my New York skepticism because I'm calling bullshit on this whole thing. I know the story of the Old Gods and the Dragons and the war you two had. I also know the Wardens are the Dragons, which means giving away thrones and kingdoms seems like charity I should be wary of. You banished us because you were afraid of us obliterating you."

This was important. I had to say "us" and keep the power on my end. In actuality, I was standing just behind the arm of the throne to hide how much my knees were shaking.

"We recognize the power of the Dragons and would like to reconcile," Alec replied as she pet her kids who were breaking out a pull-up competition of her rib cage.

"Why now?"

"Because of you, Lady Grey."

"Why me?"

Meg set both of her hands on her daggers. I wasn't sure to take this as a threat or if she was just resting. "You traveled with Morrigan. Did she tell you of the origin of the Dragons?"

"They were originally torn from the Beast. A Seven-Headed Dragon."

Gesturing to the throne, specifically to its spires, Meg told me, "Seven heads with seven horns and seven crowns. The Beast was all-powerful. A scourge in both Heaven and Hell. It could annihilate everything. That is what we *know*."

"But here is what we *think*," Alec chimed in. "The real reason the Dark Lord tore the Beast apart was because it could destroy everything, *including* him. It got too powerful. Letting the Dragons loose on us was his way of setting us against each other."

"But he didn't count on you."

I held up the burning sleeve of my robe and shook my head. "Again. Why me? I don't exactly have the best track record, ladies. I'm not some

all-powerful being here. My entire mortal life I spent dealing with weird phobias and odd allergies. I once got food poisoning from chewing gum." I threw my hands up as if they could understand this.

Alec laughed. "I will admit we reveled in killing your kind. Without your memories, and your true powers, destroying every Shade from the Fourth Circle down proved … enjoyable. But what we are searching for is much more powerful than a mere dragon. The Dark Lord would swallow a Dragon or an Old God and spit them out in an instant. But you, Lady Grey, have taken in the powers of *all* seven Shades at one point. Is this not true?"

"I—" I honestly wasn't sure. "Seven Shades? Probably only six, I guess?"

"*All* seven," Meg corrected. "You absorbed five Shades, plus your own. And the last Shade, we believe he lent you his power at some point."

D. He had fixed my injuries a few times. Had he lent me some of his power, as well? How could that be true?

The two Furies took a knee and Meg told me, "You have transcended the Dragon. You are the closest being to reforming the Beast, Lady Grey. You are the one who will help us break into the final Circle of Hell and kill the Dark Lord, now and forever."

I laughed and walked around the throne to give myself some time to think. "I'm sorry. I think my ears are not functioning down on this level. It sounded like you just asked me to waltz into the Ninth Circle of Hell and kill the origin of all darkness."

Once again, Meg was adamant. "Along with the powers you possess, you will have the strength of Pandemonium at your fingertips. The gate to the Seventh Circle is protected by a guardian—an Old God, but a sympathizer to the throne. Help us break through, and our army of one-hundred thousand fully-armed centaurs will flood into the final Circle and bring Hell to its knees."

I nodded slowly, trying to buy myself some time before I had to respond. I slipped into the throne and crossed my legs. Then, after a few seconds to think it over, I shrugged. "Cool. Are we going right now or can I have, like, ten minutes to de-frag?"

Both Furies looked at each other and then up at me.

Meg's black eyes narrowed to glowing slits. "So ... you're okay with this?"

I shrugged and looked around. "Ooh, this is nice. Cozy for a throne. You know, I don't have prior throne experience, but I would never have put the words 'cozy' and 'throne' together. I mean, it would never come into my mind. And yet, here it is. But to answer your question. Oh yeah. A-ok with this. Okay with all of it, as a matter of fact. Especially since I was kind of expecting you to, you know, threaten me somehow. Like, force me to do something. And I would have to decline. And a big fat fight would break out as I would try to escape. But I guess we're good. I was planning to go down there and stir up some hell of my own. So if that's all you want, we're all good!"

The Furies looked at each other again. "Well, that's good news. Guess we don't have to use this now."

Meg gestured to a side door I had failed to see when I walked in. Two puppets pushed open the doors and Gaffrey Palls, D, Not-Mark, and Cain were led into the room, bound in chains.

The familiar troupe looked beaten and tortured. D even had several sharp spears sticking out of his back and chest.

The demon, the angel, the liar, and the man all looked up to see me sitting in a robe of white burning flames atop the throne of Pandemonium as I sheepishly waved to them.

"Oh, hey."

THE FURIES ESCORTED us through a large gate to where they said the execution would be fitting. At their behest, a small army of centaurs flanked us.

I want to call them centaurs but in actuality, they were *opposite* of centaurs. Marching in rank and file with spears, shields, and other armaments were creatures with the heads of horses and the legs of men. With hooves for hands, they kept dropping their weapons. With their skinny human legs, they were top-heavy and clumsy. I want to say this was the dumbest army I'd ever been backed by, but it was the *only* army and I don't want to sound ungrateful. It made all the sense in the world why the Furies needed a Dragon on their side to take over Hell.

Minding our distance from those oafish creatures, I stayed close to where they kept my friends. I visited Palls first and then Cain. The ex-angel wasn't looking too good. The gray, cracked skin had spread up around her throat and shoulders, making it difficult to look at her. Lastly, there was D. Walking toward the back, we were close enough to whisper amongst ourselves.

The demon took one look at my fiery robe and shook his head. "Please tell me you have a plan, Grey."

I looked at him, offended. "Me? A plan? I was just going to use the Furies to get me down to find Petty faster. I know that sounds like a plan but I consider it more of an impulse. The same way when you're standing in line waiting to pay for something and the store's posted its blah-blah knick-knacks in front of your face for you say, 'Oh yeah. I might need triple C batteries to power that portable vibrator I got last Hanukkah.'"

D rolled his eyes—or perhaps he almost passed out. "If you're rambling again, this really means we're screwed. Is it true you killed one of the Furies back at the boat?"

"I barfed fire on her, D. Not exactly a highlight of my stay down here."

Like I had already done for Cain and Palls, I snapped one flame onto my finger and planted it right where D's hands were bound. The chain snapped and I placed the two connecting loops into his hand so that it appeared to still be whole. Up close, the spears in his body looked gross: three through the back, one through his chest, and the last through his belly. I felt like I was talking to a pincushion. "That looks bad," I told him.

"All good," he replied and coughed out a thick wad of black blood. Swallowing some of it, he added, "Never been better."

"Lady Grey," Alec called. She had no proper eyeballs so it was hard to tell how hard she was staring at my interaction with the prisoner. She beckoned me to the front of the procession with a wave of her skinny fingers.

In front of us a black staircase led down into a field of red clay and rocks. Heat was pouring up from this space and I was reluctant to walk down. I turned to Meg, who was watching me carefully, and asked, "What's this?"

"This is the Seventh Circle," she answered.

As soon as I took my first steps down, the heat seemed to climb right onto me. I'm fairly certain that when someone came up with the phrase, "This place is hot as Hell" they had just come from a short stay in the Seventh Circle.

This was the most barren and desolate area of the afterlife I had come to know. The ground was red sand, the sky was charred and filled with flaming meteors, and the air was filled with debris. The only thing I could see ahead was a mountain with a large smoking chimneystack sticking out of it.

Suddenly there was a sound coming from behind us and a second

army filed in alongside our sorry looking horde. Leading thousands of camera-headed Followers, spear-lugging rats in chainmail, and a large contingent of trolls was Hel. She wore black armor and what I thought was a scepter, but as she starting speaking into it, I saw it was just a spiked selfie-stick.

"Hel-Heads. We have come to liberate the Inferno," she shouted, and her army roared in unison.

"What is she doing here?" I asked.

Meg bowed. "We have made a pact. Only with our armies combined can we retake Hell." Even as she said this, the Fury grimaced at the look of Hel's army, namely the ordinary-looking men and boys just standing around looking bored. "What are those things supposed to be?"

"This is my legion," Hel answered proudly. "An army of unstoppable trolls."

From out of the group—and it was hard to tell from whom—one of them shouted, "This is just like that scene from *The Lord of the Rings* with the goblin army, only stupider."

A second voice replied, "Uruk-Hai. Whoever called them goblins should go kill themself."

"Shut up!" Hel spat and cleared her throat. "Let's just get this over with."

The two Furies walked with me as a group of backward centaurs kept the rest of the party behind.

"We call for an audience," Meg shouted. Using her four wings to hover and Alec keeping her children close, I could tell the Furies were scared of what was to come. If whoever lived on top of that mountain was powerful enough to rattle even the Furies, what chance did I have?

"We call for an audience." This time it was Alec who shouted. But the meteors still fell. And the wind still whipped. And the heat just fucking killed everything.

"We call—"

"YOU CALL?" a voice boomed. "YOU CALL?"

The smoke pouring out of the smokestack flushed into the sky and somehow made this sorry pit even hotter. Then a piece of the mountain

the size of a New York City block bent off from the rest and flew into the air. It swooped over us, ultimately breaking its end into five stubbed pieces that collided with the smokestack. Drawing it from the mountain, a set of lips puckered underneath it as it blew more spoke into the atmosphere.

"YOU CALL TO YOUR DEATH IF YOU CALL HERE."

The ground shook as this monstrous creature, the one I had confused for a mountain, rolled over onto its stomach and clenched a mighty cigar between its bus-sized fingers. It had the face of a bull crowned in a massive mane, most of which was made into tight braids using ropes. It sported highly-defined muscles, each with carvings of symbols scarred into its black flesh. The two horns on its head were pierced with hoops you could park a few cars in. It was a Minotaur large enough to accidentally inhale me.

"We've only come to talk," Meg called to it.

The Minotaur scoffed and nearly blew us away in the process. "LET'S TALK ABOUT HOW YOU KEEP BRINGING ME THINGS AND I KEEP MAKING MESSES OF THEM. LET'S TALK ABOUT *THAT*."

Resting its snout on its folded arms, the monster squinted at me. "THIS ONE IS SMALL. I'VE FOUND MIGHTIER THINGS IN MY DROPPINGS."

Meg stepped between us. "This isn't a Dragon to kill. She is on our side. Our offer still stands. Throw down this fruitless calling. You do not need to do his bidding. Ever since he came back, he has done nothing but poison Pandemonium and the rest of Hell."

Slamming its palms on the ground to silence us with an earthquake, the Minotaur rose up onto his hooves. It was easily taller than the apartment building my parents raised me in.

"I DUNNO," it said, half-humored. "I KINDA LIKE WHAT HE DID TO THE PLACE."

The colossal Minotaur flicked his cigar and it landed so many miles away that I lost sight of the butt. Scooping up a few stacked trees it had by its hooves, it held the end in the air and, using a flaming meteor, lit the end to its new stogie.

"LOOK AROUND. I USED TO GUARD THIS PLACE, THIS

CESSPOOL. *HE* LET ME DESTROY EVERYTHING HERE. *HE* LET ME KILL EVERYONE. THE SEVENTH CIRCLE IS NOTHING MORE THAN WHAT YOU SEE BEFORE YOU AND I'M ITS LONE SURVIVOR. NOW, IF WE'RE DONE TALKING HERE, I NEED TO GO FIND MY MURDERING CLUB, WHERE DID I PUT THAT THING?"

I felt two taps on my shoulder and both Meg and Alec were backing off.

"All yours from here, Lady Grey."

"Yes. Good luck, Lady Dragon."

As the Minotaur struggled to find its weapon, I chased after them. "You didn't say anything about fighting something that can wipe its ass with Long Island."

"Kill it so our armies can invade. Or do you want us to hurt your friends?"

"I choose neither," I yelled and snapped both of my fingers at them. Expecting the attack, the two Furies dodged as a torrent of sustained black fire singed the ground in both directions. A few feet away, I saw the blasts had at least sent the ass backward-centaurs into a panic (the brain parts were also horse), giving Palls all the breathing room he needed. Breaking out of his chains, he freed Cain and grabbed D—who was still unfit to fight—and came running toward me with Not-Mark at his heels.

"HERE IT IS," bellowed the Minotaur as it found its murdering club.

The Furies circled around and started clamoring for their army to reform and attack us, while, ahead of us, the minotaur took a long drag from its cigar while propping up a beaten club the size of a small housing complex onto its shoulder.

With his bare hands, Palls tore the black spears from D's body and pushed him to stand.

"All right, Grey. What next?"

"Why does everyone think I have a plan?" But even as I said this, watching the creature walk toward us and seeing the Fury's armies set their ranks gave me an idea. A terrible one, but a plan nonetheless.

"We'll only get one try at this. It looks like it'll take forever for it to swing that thing. All we need to do is hit that club with everything we got, all of us. If it breaks, we should be free. If not, at least it might get off balance. Either way, we run past it and into the gate."

But Palls said, "That's not going to work. I heard the Furies talk already. That gate behind it is locked and only the Minotaur has the strength to open it."

D pushed the blue man forward and Not-Mark pointed. "Another entrance. A tunnel just to the side. That's where I came up."

With everyone looking to me for approval, and the Minotaur slipping the cigar into its mouth to grip his club with two hands, and the Fury's army now charging, I shouted, "Sure! This isn't going to suck at all."

The next thing I knew, the club was coming down on us. It was so large it cast a dark shadow both on our tiny party and the entire army behind us.

Cain let her wings out and summoned her god of death scythe.

Palls formed a massive hellfire ball so large he could barely contain it with both hands.

Burning chains sprouted out of D's body, which he wrapped around his arms like armor.

Not-Mark pleaded for his life.

My hellfire gown flared and raw energy poured out of me, nearly blowing my friends away in the process. Forming a small sun in my hand, I wound back to pitch.

This was it—all or nothing. I wasn't planning on dying here, not when I was so close to seeing Petty again.

The mighty weapon came down just as we attacked it with everything we had.

The moment our blows met the club, a sonic shockwave spread from the point of impact in a ring. The sky changed. The ground rumbled. The gathered armies and even the Furies were scattered to the wind as hellfire and ash flew everywhere. A small tornado formed. Lightning struck random places around us.

The club didn't break, but the blast from our combined efforts tore the Minotaur's whole arm clean off of its torso. The monster roared as its severed limb sailed over its horned head, still clenching the club.

With our chance in front of us, we dashed between its staggering legs and made for the small edge of the curved gate shaped like an all-seeing eye. Just as quickly as it appeared, the fiery cloak began to dissipate as I ran until it was nothing more than tiny pockets of flame that blew out in the wind.

Not-Mark saw to it that we spotted the crack he was about to climb into and dove in, his blue ass vanishing through a space I would have never guessed was possible.

Cain went next.

Just as it was my turn, I spun around to make sure D and Palls were close behind. But what I saw instead was another mammoth shadow closing in from the sky. We hadn't taken into account how fast the monster could recover and the rage it would feel for losing a limb. Palls and D were looking up at the Minotaur's fist as it came to down to crush us, but it was Palls who acted first. He shoved D into me, knocking the two of us off balance, and then crammed both of our dumbfounded bodies into the secret tunnel.

I fell backward but recovered in time to see Palls take a step back. The tunnel was too tight for the three of us to climb into and he knew it.

Still, I shouted "Palls!" and stretched out my hand for him.

He stuffed his into his pockets. "She's not down here, Grey," he shouted with a smirk. And then the fist landed like an atom bomb.

Gaffrey Palls was gone, punctuated by an explosion outside the cave entrance that brought most of it down around our heads.

25

Tons of boulders and rocks had fallen around my shoulders, chest, and waist. This, coupled with the fact I had just seen Palls void out in front of me, made my body not want to move. It was dark and most of my energy felt like it was seeping from me. I was also cold, which was bizarre since the Seventh Circle was a burning wasteland.

Being trapped beneath the rocks and stones did nothing for the emotional pain that was hammering through my joints and chest. I never thought I would shed a tear for Gaffrey Palls, but there I was, crying my eyes out. I had blamed him for many things, maybe even a few he had no control over. He was a friend, a reluctant one, for sure, but he was there. Out of all the people in the world that understood what I had gone through—losing my sister, putting up with manipulative angels and Shades, living my life with crippling anxiety—Gaffrey Palls knew it all too well.

Mustering my strength—and almost as if hearing him groan about the time I was wasting—I decided not to spend too much of it mourning the guy. He had saved me more times than I could count, and we had turned out to be closer than I ever thought imaginable, but I still had a job to do. If I turned into one big, blubbery mess, Palls' sacrifice would be for nothing. This is what I told myself as I reached out and started moving debris with my bare hands. With the strength that had flowed through me against the Minotaur now gone, I dug and clawed my way through what I felt was a tomb—one I denied with every fiber in me.

A few minutes in, I found a small tunnel to follow. Still, I had to ground my elbows into my ribs to fit, and the walls were so close around me that my grunts and cries crashed in my own ears, but I continued.

For Palls.

For my sister.

The further I dug, the colder it became. Taking this as a sign I was on the right track, I tugged on a jutting piece of stone a little too fast, and the ceiling started to crumble down around me. I didn't stay still to get crushed this time, but set my hands onto a slab that folded over and revealed a wave of blue light.

Two sets of hands reached in and grabbed me.

Hitting the ground around Cain and D, the tunnel behind me vanished under the crumbling weight.

My whole body ached, and from the looks of it, Cain and D were in the same condition. Not-Mark didn't even wait for us to say our hellos or catch a second wind. He pointed behind him and beckoned us to follow.

"Hurry now. We've made it to the Eighth Circle."

The Circle was freezing and dark, making it easily the most morbid place in all of Hell. The Circle itself was a dark cavern with sharp stalactites hanging overhead. There were pits connected by large land bridges, but there was nothing in them. A few bloodstains, some scattered weapons, but there wasn't a single soul in the entire Eighth Circle.

"Grey," D started but then stopped. I knew what he wanted to say.

"He wasn't a jackass," I declared sternly so that he knew this was the extent of conversation I wanted us to have about Gaffrey Palls. And then to our liar, I asked, "What happened to this place?"

"He let everyone loose," he replied nervously. "He knocked down the walls here first. He let loose the seducers and the philanderers and the guys who sold ultra-absorbent towels. Then he freed me, and a few dozen others, from the frozen lake. It's nearby and that's where the cold comes from. We are close."

As much as I hated to admit, once again, the liar was telling the truth. Spanning in front of us was a massive lake, its entire one-hundred-yard surface frozen like perfect glass. Turning around, I could see the door shaped like an eye just beyond the pits we had crossed. In front of us, across the lake, was a single metal door. Nothing elaborate or ornate. Human-sized. Ordinary.

"Is that it?"

"That's where he left when he freed me," the liar explained.

Before I could ask what we should do now, Not-Mark started walking across the lake. The surface was slick, so our trek slowed to only a few feet per minute. And it only got stranger when we saw where our guide had been freed.

Toward the center, we spotted other naked blue people, which in and of itself is weird, but their bodies were completely wedged into the ice. Some were planted face first with their naked asses in the air, others sat with their heads and mouths sticking out of the surface. It didn't help they all talked.

"Mandy," one cried. "Mandy, it's me. Your dad. Is that you?"

My body nearly split as it tensed up.

"Careful, Grey. These are liars," D warned.

"Oh yeah." Exhaling, I kicked that frozen guy in the forehead for good measure.

"Kick me!" screamed one.

"Don't kick me," begged another.

"Look at my face," called someone else. "You have to agree, I have a kickable face."

I retreated as the shouts came from all over the lake. "What's their problem?"

Not-Mark called back to us. "We are bound here. Locked here. We see lies. Live lies. Now we only seek punishment. Punishment that will never come."

We were almost at the exact center of the lake when the first explosions began. Behind us, I could hear something pounding against that eye door we had bypassed, causing large chunks of the cave's ceiling to come down around us.

Cain leapt into the air and hovered there. "It's either the armies or the minotaur. Either way, we aren't going to make it if they bust down that door." She wasn't looking or speaking to me at all.

D grabbed me by the shoulders to say something, but I cut him off.

"No!"

"She's right."

"No!"

"Grey, you know that I—"

"Save it."

Another loud explosion.

D looked up at Cain. "I'll catch up."

Cain tossed me a short salute. "Be sure to tell Petty I still consider her the cuter sister."

The gray, cracked skin was now into her scalp and had taken up most of her face. Her left eye was completely black. This was her last stand and we both knew it. Calling out her sacred weapon, the ex-angel of death spun it behind her back and took off toward the direction of the banging.

D looked back at me. "Gre—"

"Don't 'Grey' me. Don't."

He put his forehead against mine. "I have to tell you something and I just need you to listen. Grey, I—"

But I pushed him aside and started walking away. "If it's that important, come tell me in person. When we've saved Petty. When this whole shit is done. Tell me to my face."

I didn't turn around. Soon after, I heard the sound of D's footsteps running against the ice toward mortal danger.

My voice cracking and my hands shaking, I told our liar to hurry it up and we took off as well.

A few minutes into our sliding/sprint, the sound of the door imploding echoed through the cavern. We had made it two-thirds of the way across and it was impossible to see how Cain and D were faring, and who they were faring their best against. It was also tough to figure out how much time we had left before that threat would catch up to us.

Not-Mark lagged behind. When I called to him, he was staring into an empty hole. It didn't take me long to figure out whose hole this was and what the blue guy had in mind.

"You're going back in? But you're free!"

"Liars are never free."

"But," I looked around at the other heads shouting nearby. "You've never lied. This entire time. You've never lied to me. Your name really is Mark, isn't it?"

Real-Mark blinked and smiled, but soon even that faltered. "The only time I lied, Amanda Grey, the only time I lied to you. Back on the boat. I told you I was freed because I thought I deserved to be." He wiped his nose with his arm. "I'm sorry," he said, cramming his body back into the ice crevice. "You should go now. He is just behind the gate."

I could hear voices echoing around. People screaming. The Hel and the Furies' army were approaching.

Leaving him behind, I ran.

Leaving Cain.

Leaving D.

Leaving Palls.

They did this all for me. All for me.

When I reached the other side of the lake and crossed onto solid ground, just ten feet from the door to my sister, I fell. The pain in me swelled and in my rage, I slammed both of my fists down so hard I felt like I'd broken them both. Crying uncontrollably, I drew myself up to my knees, but still couldn't pick my head up. Sliding my cheek along the dirt, I could see it. The door. The door was right there. I had lost everything to get here. I had lost my father. I had seen my friends run off to die. All for this. All for this moment.

Get the fuck up, I told myself. And that's what I did. I pushed with everything I had—with everything I knew—and it felt like I was tearing at time and space itself. I threw myself against the metal door. The misery I felt burned away and I swallowed the sobs as soon as they tried to start again.

I wiped my face.

I fixed my jeans and shirt.

I stood upright.

Then I kicked open the door to the Ninth and final Circle of Hell.

Considering the dead fields, the corpse sea, the arid deserts, and the sprawling cities I had experienced in Hell, the final Circle of Hell was nothing to write home about. The space was only a single chamber.

The walls were made of jagged black rocks that reached high into the air and the floors were dark and smooth. Sitting in the center of the chamber, I could see the back of an oversized throne made of various bones—human, demon, and animal. The throne was huge, almost for a creature ten or eleven feet tall, and it faced the far wall where there sat the biggest fireplace I had ever seen—roughly the size of a goalie net, maybe bigger. Inside, the flames danced back and forth like they had minds of their own.

Suddenly, the only door to the chamber slammed shut. I heard the spinning of metal and chains. Whatever was waiting for me in here didn't want me to leave.

There was no ceiling above my head, only an endless opening that vanished into a portal of white light. Along the walls, I spotted circular enclaves where Screeches nested. There must have been millions of them. Some were napping. Others were waiting to be sent off to spread strife.

Other than the snapping fire and the freakish birds softly buzzing to themselves, the whole place was shrouded in silence. I could hear my breathing. My footsteps. This chamber was vast and also empty.

No Petty.

No Dark Lord.

I was alone.

At least I thought so until I spotted the leg dangling over of the arm of the throne.

"Amanda Grey."

It was the last voice I ever thought I would hear again, but I recognized it immediately.

Barnem the ex-Seraphim brought his head out from behind the throne and smiled so hard his cheeks touched the edges of his eyes. Hopping to his feet, he walked around where I could see him. He was still wearing the armored chest piece from the last time we clashed. His arms were exposed and his left hand sported a silver gauntlet. The white wings on his back had been burnt down to black stubs. Waving daintily, he tossed me a "Wassup."

"What the hell is going on here, Barnem?"

"What the hell, indeed, Grey. What the Hell, indeed."

"Where's Petty?"

He was about to shrug, but I took a step toward him. The ex-angel backed away and laughed. "Okay, okay. She's not here."

"Why not? And why are *you* here?"

Barnem sighed and hopped up on the throne. "You know, when I got here, they wanted to torture me. Because of you, I had my soul tainted by those abominations and got sent down here. Because of *you*! So I asked to see a manager. And I found myself right down here—in this room which no one in Hell had opened in several thousand centuries—and guess what I found?" He knocked on the throne. "Absolutely nothing. There was no one here."

"That's impossible," I told him. "Someone called Petty down here."

Barnem waved a finger at me. "Oh, that was me. You see, I couldn't let an opportunity like this pass. This place was left without a leader. And you know what they say, Grey: 'Better to rule in Hell ...' etcetera, etcetera. Ooh, hey! Want to check out the new sound system I got hooked up in this place? I use it to drown out all of the human suffering."

Fetching a tiny remote from his pocket, Barnem pressed a button and the chamber was filled with the sound of death metal blasting through invisible speakers. After a few seconds, he shut it off and looked at me as if I should be impressed.

I shook my head. "You're the one who's been fucking everything up down here? You're the reason why all of Hell's this way?"

"Fucking every—" Barnem crossed his arms. "Grey, I don't know if you've noticed, but this is Hell. It's a haven for the wicked and sullied. All I did was introduce advertisements, civil unrest, and a highly obnoxious font. So what if the whole place just falls apart? Good riddance. I can annihilate Hell and still serve my higher power even if the big wigs don't recognize it."

"You haven't changed one bit, Barnem. You're still the guy who farts on an escalator. You create the problem and everyone else has to deal with it."

Disgusted, the angel scoffed at me. "You know what they call me down here? You want to know? A 'Falling Star.' Well, fuck them! Let's see what's really falling when this whole goddamn institution caves in around them. I mean, that's what my original plan was. But then...." The Seraph's eyes locked onto me. "Then I heard your sister was down here and I thought, I might as well torture her while I'm here."

I snapped my fingers, but no fires started. I tried three and four and five times. Nothing.

Barnem sighed and patted the chair of bones. "Your little lightshow won't work here, I'm afraid. See, as long as I'm touching this throne, I have the power of the Dark Lord. And I can say you can't do a damn thing to me and that's what it'll have to be."

"Petty."

Barnem sneered. "I knew you would come if I took her. That demon friend of yours had called her up, but I called her back down, all the way down, and you took the bait. I had wanted you to void out on your way down, but you are the corn wedged in the gums of my timeline, Amanda Grey."

I sucked my teeth. "I would typically call that a compliment, Barnem, but now it just sounds like you want to make out with me. So how about this? Powers or not, I'm going to go over there and start punching you. I'm going to continue punching you as hard as I can and for as long as I can until you tell me what you did with my sister."

"Aha." Barnem shrugged. "But I'm going to tell you anyway. You see, Grey, that's the whole point. I brought your sister down here to kill both Greys at once. But then she was called up. She's not here."

"Bullshit," I shouted. "I've been through every Circle. I've fought every demon and Old God to get down here and now you're saying she went back up? To what Circle? Who called her?"

The Seraph pointed straight up. "No Circle, Grey. Your sister went all the way up. She went to Heaven. Some may call it a last-minute miracle. To me, it sounded like someone did you a favor."

I stood there stunned for a few seconds. I looked around. I checked Barnem's face. Then I just started laughing. That was the only reaction I could anchor myself to, so I just laughed and laughed. I laughed so much my cheeks hurt, that I fell ass-first onto the ground, howling. Soon, my wide-mouth cackling bled into actual sobs. And from those sobs came the tears.

I had survived Hell—survived torture—and seen the destruction of an entire afterlife. I had witnessed the death of my friends—the ones that had taken me an entire lifetime-plus to make. I had missed my father's passing and had not been there to console my mother. I had even connected with someone (or something?) in a way that made it painful to see him leave. All of this and my little sister was saved in the Eleventh Hour.

The favor. The request I sent with those freaky-looking angels. It had taken forever to kick in, but it had worked. Petty had been saved at the last possible moment. She was safe.

Outside the chamber came the sound of the ice lake splitting. An unstoppable army was on our doorstep.

Barnem blinked. "So I brought you both down here to look into your pained faces as I killed the both of you. But now I can't. I'll admit, kind of bummed right now. Talk about a letdown."

I could hear voices shouting just outside the metal door.

Wiping the tears from my eyes, I gathered myself and crossed my legs. "You know they're going to kill you, Barnem."

"Probably." He looked genuinely unbothered by the idea. Then he held up his hand with the gauntlet and removed the metal glove. There was no hand inside, just a gray cracked stump. Barnem was dying.

"I knew that by refusing to defile myself like the rest, I would have a short time here. That's why I came down. To make my mark. But then there's this empty room, this empty throne." He tossed the gauntlet onto the ground. "I don't know what any of this means. Or why the Old Gods and the dragons were allowed to battle. Or anything, really. It's all some bigger plan I can neither see nor give two shits about. It's all just prophecy wrapped in prophecy double dipped in the chewy nougat of another prophecy,"

"I see you still have that food fetish," I told Barnem and he just shrugged.

The Furies were giving their final marching orders. I wondered what had happened to D and Cain. Still on the ground, I took some satisfaction in knowing all of this wasn't a waste.

"You know, Barnem. One of my major takeaways from this whole 'Hell' experience is that I'm kind of a fuck up. I say the wrong things; I punch the wrong people. My life is stitched together by one mistake after another. But I can honestly say I'm totally okay with all of it because I'm 2-0 against your schemes."

Barnem exhaled and sat on the edge of the throne. "If we're both being honest here, part of me is looking forward to what's going to happen next. Not for myself, of course. I stand before you hoping to stay alive long enough to see them decapitate you and make blood angels out of your guts. That's part of me. But then there's another part of me. You've heard me tell you that 'Hell is other people.'" Barnem leaned his head back and stared into the light. "I was always quick to agree with that statement. Hell is other people, I thought. Humans, angels, demons … everyone. Hell was everyone else. But that's not true. Hell isn't other people."

Barnem, the ex-Seraphim, stared right into my eyes, and said, "It's just *you*. You, Amanda Grey. Because even in the afterlife, you find a way to fuck with my plans."

With my hand over my heart, I closed my eyes. "Thank you. That means a lot to me. And, since we're getting sentimental here, and it seems we're both going to die, what do you say to one for the road? For old time's sake?"

I flashed him one of my fists.

Something heavy crashed into the chamber door. It was holding, but by the sound of it, the steel couldn't take another blow.

The Seraph smirked. "The last time I gave you a free shot, you stabbed me in the face. But … what the hell, right?" In a familiar pose, Barnem leaned forward, exposing his chin.

But as soon as I took a step forward to punch him one last time, he yelled, "Sike."

The ground beneath my feet instantly turned to black tar and ten large arms grew out of the murk. Stretching like taffy, they began snaking up my arms and legs and dragging me into the darkness. I fought with everything I had, but their holds were impossible to break. With my lower half now under, and my mouth clasped shut by one of the summoned hands, Barnem stooped down to where I could see him.

"As much as I want to see you die here, I came up with a better plan. You see, my mistake was thinking Hell would be the perfect place to torture you. But I guess I forgot who I was dealing with here. Not you. Not Amanda Grey." He smiled. "So I'm sending you to the only place where you will *really* be tortured. I'm not sending you alone, either. Call it a parting gift between two old ex-neighbors."

Just as the door to the throne room collapsed and snarling cries filled the chamber, Barnem waved a farewell and I was dragged underneath. All I saw was black.

And then white.

And then green.

Teal, blue, burgundy, tan.

Opening my eyes, I found myself sitting in a green chair with a knitted pillow built into the backrest. D was beside me in a seat of his own, looking bloodied and just as confused as I must have looked.

Barnem had sent both of us into a room with four walls. Wood paneling framed the ceiling where a blue sky with white clouds had been painted. There were just the two chairs, a lone wooden door, and us.

The first thing D did when he leapt from his chair was launch into an excuse as to why he left me back in the Eighth Circle.

The first thing I did to shut him up was kiss him.

I can't say this was the original plan I had when I saw him again, but it was what I wanted. And the two of us stayed there, enjoying the kiss for as long as time would have us.

By my estimate, that was about fifteen seconds.

The wooden door burst open and creatures flushed into the space. Bears that walked upright, people with eagle heads, folks with cat ears and paws. They ran right at us and some of them were armed.

D and I separated in time to start throwing hellfire around the place like it was a performance art project. His chains whipped around in one deadly arc, beheading a few of the bears. This scattered some of the eagle people flying around the ceiling, but I burned them out of the sky and let their ashes rain down on us.

We gutted, beheaded, roasted, and wedgied every single creature that came at us in the small room. Fighting alongside D was definitely not the way I wanted to tell him how I felt about him, but for some reason, it felt like the perfect way, too.

When it was all said and done, the two of us had laid waste to an entire horde of freaks. We had killed everyone except a bear-man whose entire back was currently being eaten by hellfire. He ran around the room screaming, trying to stop, drop, and roll, but finding it impossible with all of the smoking corpses on the floor. He opted for running out of the room and nearly bumped into a man and woman that were walking in at the time.

Rocking nametags with their names written in thick green marker, and with one holding what looked like a vanilla sheet cake served on a pristine silver tray, the two familiar folks stopped just a few feet from us, horrified.

Around us, the room was partially on fire and the air was thick with the smell of burnt feathers and fur.

Donaldson and Petty took off their glittery party hats as my sister cleared her throat.

"Hey … Mandy. Uh, welcome to Heaven?"

THE END...FOR NOW

ABOUT THE AUTHOR

Alcy Leyva is a Bronx-born writer, teacher, and pizza enthusiast. He graduated from Hunter College with a B.A. in English (Creative Writing) and received an MFA in Fiction from The New School. Alcy enjoys writing personal essays, poetry, short fiction, book reviews, and film analysis, but is also content with practicing standing so still that he will someday slip through time and space. He lives in New York with his wife and a small army of male heirs.